Cottage
by the
Creek

a birch harbor novel

ELIZABETH

#4 JH

COTTAGE BY THE CREEK
Publishing in the Pines
White Mountains, Arizona

*For all the teachers in my life. My husband, my parents, my
brother and sister, grandparents, cousins, friends... the list goes on.*

CHAPTER 1—CLARA

There was nothing worse than being the new girl at school.

And Miss Clara Hannigan wasn't exempt.

When, just weeks earlier, Clara learned that she had to transfer from teaching eighth grade to teaching ninth, she'd balked.

And not because she was scared to teach high school or work in a new building.

Not because she was afraid to start over.

She was nervous because in reality, Clara was *not* starting over at all.

She would be the new teacher at Birch Harbor High, yes. But she'd have mostly the same students as she did the year before.

With one or two notable exceptions.

Now that Labor Day was firmly in the rearview mirror, summer had burned away. So too had all the fresh starts of the Hannigan sisters.

Finally, normal life was settling in. Kate with her Inn.

Amelia with her lighthouse. And Megan with her matchmaking and events business.

One might say Clara also had found fresh footing in the cottage by the creek, the home that she'd nearly lost just two seasons prior. And perhaps by September, Clara also might settle into her new position, too. She'd attended the teacher in-services. She'd set up her classroom and written the bell schedule on the chalkboard (the one the maintenance staff refused to replace).

But the best thing about new beginnings, usually, was that the person who was enjoying the new beginning was enjoying it based on her own drive. The fact that *she* brought about a fresh start. *She* made a change in her life.

For Clara, though, her so-called new beginning was happening *to* her. In spite of her, actually.

Nevertheless, she managed to roll with the punches, taking the evenings to clean the cottage and sort through her mother's old things. She didn't quite have the surplus money to redecorate, but even just folding tired afghans and tucking them high up in the linen closet was a start.

So that's what she did: stowed the past in order to make room for the future. It's all she could do, really.

Presently, Clara unlocked the hall entry door at the far end of her wing and slipped inside. In one hand, her canvas teacher tote which read *I'm silently correcting your grammar.* Inside of the tote was her thin, insulated lunchbox and her daily planner. Come that afternoon, however, it would be filled with students' first assignments, extra paperwork, perhaps a lesson-planning book, too.

In the other hand, Clara carried a rose-gold Thermos gifted to her by her department chair. Normally, she'd already had enough coffee to forgo bringing more to school. But now that she lived alone, Clara figured it'd be a good idea to change some things up. She didn't need to worry about waking her mother, so she could set the coffee after getting up. She could blow dry her hair and unfold the rusty, creaky ironing board to press out wrinkles in her First Day of School outfit. She could pour herself a Thermos of coffee and carry it to work like a true professional, not a teenager playing schoolteacher.

Once inside her classroom, Clara popped into the supply closet she shared with the teacher next door. There, she carefully stowed her lunchbox in the mini fridge and shelved her tote.

One hour remained before the first bell, which gave her enough time to neatly lay out name cards on each desk—regardless of how old the students were or how well she already knew them, a seating chart would be Clara's best weapon in managing the class' behavior.

After that, she dutifully carried her roster to the front podium, then turned to the lone white board on a narrow stretch of wall space in the corner of the room. This was, no doubt, the school's attempt to modernize. She selected a crisp, purple dry erase marker, fresh out of its package, and set about detailing her agenda for the First Day of School.

1. *Welcome*
2. *Ice-breaker*
3. *Housekeeping (syllabus and attendance)*
4. *Story Writing*
5. *Dismissal*

She paced backwards until she bumped into the first row of desks, then studied the deep, inky letters. A light sweat formed at the small of her back as Clara tried to visualize how first period would go.

There were complications, no doubt, to this new teaching assignment.

She'd have to face a couple of students she'd almost failed the year before. And their *parents*, too, eventually.

She'd have to prove her worth as a *high school level* English teacher to children-turned-teenagers who only ever knew her as the young *middle school language arts* teacher.

Then, when Mercy Hennings arrived, tidy leather backpack straps throttled in her nervous fists, Clara would have to pretend that she was *not* going on a date with Jake Hennings that Saturday. Jake, the handsome widower who just so happened to be Clara's favorite student's father.

And, most threateningly perhaps, Clara would be in charge of Viviana Fiorillo for an hour and a half every day. Viviana, the independent Queen Bee who needed no supervision. The ethereal, beachy beauty of Heirloom Island.

The daughter of Clara's *father*, mind you.

Clara turned and tweaked the desks she'd knocked out of place, her gaze falling across the room as a stomachache settled into place.

Perhaps it didn't matter if Clara was the one who made the changes in her life or if she was simply the victim of them. It didn't matter if she didn't instigate her own destiny like her older, wiser sisters.

Perhaps Clara just needed to survive the school year.

CHAPTER 2—KATE

"She didn't want to take your boat?" Kate stood at the seawall that stretched across the backyard of the Heirloom Inn, her hand shielding her eyes from the sun. Matt Fiorillo was on the other end of the phone line, waiting anxiously to get confirmation that his ninth-grade daughter Viviana was safely en route ashore.

It was early morning, the first day of school for all of Birch Harbor Unified. Kate could picture all the mothers in town—the mothers with school-aged children. That first day back was a joyous occasion, by all accounts.

Mostly, or at least for Kate's grown sons, the return to school was a return to normalcy. Routines took their old effect, and friends and the promise of a thirty-minute lunch padded the fall for kids as their moms set about conjuring elaborate to-do lists only to fall asleep on the sofa by ten in the morning.

Now, dating a single dad, Kate could taste that excitement all over again, on his behalf... and hers.

"I guess the ferry is cooler than my Bayliner," Matt replied.

As the sun hauled itself above the eastern horizon, Kate spotted it—the Harbor Ferry edging along placid sunny waters toward the marina. Matt had been nervous about the whole thing, but Viviana insisted he stay home and not boat over from the Island until the coast was clear.

"I'm sure she just wanted to be independent. A private boat is normally much cooler than the public school ferry." Kate had to laugh to herself at her reply to him. In what universe did school children ride a ferry before hopping on a bus to get to school?

In Birch Harbor, Michigan, of course... at least, if the child lived on Heirloom Island and didn't want to be home-schooled for grades nine through twelve. Which most children out there did not. They'd spent the better part of their lives cooped up on the tiny stretch of land floating on Lake Huron. They were ready for bigger things.

Even Nora Hannigan, Kate's own mother, had been through the drill. Having attended St. Mary's of the Isle Catholic School, she rode the ferry the other way—*to* Heirloom Island rather than from it.

But that was years ago.

Now the new guard was moving in, and comprising it was a set of teenage girls sure to bring a little life back into Kate Hannigan's world.

CHAPTER 3—AMELIA

A melia sat at her kitchen table alone, the yearbook Clara had discovered splayed in front of her. Just the day before, she'd been sitting there, reading her sister's text.

What it all meant was still unclear, but as Amelia carefully shuffled through the pages, she recounted everything she knew:

One: Nora Hannigan had a teenage affair with Gene Carmichael, resulting in the birth and subsequent adoption of a baby girl, now named Liesel Hart. Liesel lived in Hickory Grove, Indiana and wanted little (if anything) to do with her birth father, since she never knew Gene Carmichael *was* her birth father.

Which brought Amelia to number two: Liesel Hart spent her entire life under the assumption that, in fact, Wendell Acton was her birth father, on the grounds that Liesel learned Nora Hannigan was her birth mother. This complicated the Hannigan-Acton will in that the lighthouse didn't stay in the family until Amelia (with Michael-the-Lawyer's help) earned back the deed from a generous-if-disinterested Liesel.

Three: Gene Carmichael didn't move on emotionally from Nora, but she moved on from him and went on to fall head over heels for local lighthouse rat Wendell. All was well in the marriage until the summer of 1992, when their eldest daughter (Amelia's sister, Kate) fell pregnant just as Nora had years and years before. The conflict from that point was muddy. Nora wanted to completely hide the pregnancy and rear Clara as her own, which she had. Wendell had been softer about the whole thing. After all, Amelia recalled him saying, *It's 1992! Not 1942!* Still, he maintained his allegiance to Nora, going so far as to bend to her will about building a hideaway house by the creek to keep the pregnancy secret for his wife and daughters and help to keep intact whatever reputation she thought they had.

Then, *poof*. He was gone. After Amelia and her mother and sisters came back from an extended vacation to Arizona, Wendell was gone. Police records were scant and unhelpful, and very little evidence of how local law enforcement conducted their search remained. Just the standard missing person's report with two subsequent follow-up reports. Both devoid of new information.

His last will and testament, however, survived through Nora. And in it, he bequeathed his firearm and wedding band, both of which were still missing. Also, his watch, which they'd found by a miracle on the dock out back of the lighthouse.

But that wasn't all that still existed regarding ol' Wendell.

Amelia had unearthed four newspaper articles, tucked neatly in the bowels of the lighthouse.

The first: *Local father and husband missing from lighthouse area.*

The second: *Hannigan family implicated in disappearance of local man.*

The third: *Wendell Acton left town. Case closed.*

And the last, an apparently unrelated Op-Ed: *How to nurture your marriage. Ten tips from local wives who get it right.*

Nestled inside of that final column? A name that didn't sit well with Amelia—Judith Carmichael.

And that tidbit drew her back to the fourth thing she'd learned: Gene Carmichael went as far as to move to Birch Harbor for several years, apparently in pursuit of Nora, who never did return his advances. Eventually, he met and married a fellow educator by the name of Judith Banks. Judith came from Heirloom Island, but together she and Gene bobbed between Birch Harbor, Heirloom Island, and elsewhere in Michigan until he convinced her to dock their houseboat back in Birch Harbor for the weekends, allowing them freedom to be tourist-locals, a rare combination.

Apparently, Judith enjoyed this slice of life and took up with the town council as a summer representative. Amelia didn't quite grasp Judith's role or how she set about fulfilling it beyond the searing recent rejection of Megan's match-making and events business.

And that's where Amelia found herself hung up. Confused.

With Judith Carmichael, who now apparently bore a deeper connection to the Hannigan women.

Because according to Nora's dusty, water-stained year-book, Nora and Judith had been classmates at St. Mary's of the Isle on Heirloom Island. Long before Judith offered advice on *getting it right* as a wife. Long before either Nora or Judith ever met the men they would one day marry.

Now Amelia needed to figure out what that connection meant.

If anything.

CHAPTER 4—MEGAN

Megan Stevenson stood behind her seventeen-year-old daughter in front of the full-length mirror behind her bedroom door.

"You look perfect. Let's go take your first-day photo." A family tradition, Megan always looked forward to getting prints made of each first-day-of-school photo to add to the collage she'd started way back when Sarah began pre-K.

"I can't believe I'm getting ready for school *here*," Sarah said. Her tone was more wondrous than whiney, but it was a dart to Megan's heart. Neither one of them would have preferred that Sarah enter her last year of high school in a two-bedroom apartment in a new town.

But there they were, a family at least, starting fresh in Birch Harbor. Megan offered her daughter a compassionate smile and replied, "I'm a little homesick, too. But Dad has the contractors out at the field this week. Who knows? Maybe by Christmas, we'll be in our new house, and we'll feel a little more situated."

It was a stretch, but if weather didn't become too big an obstacle, and if Megan's husband (yes—husband, not ex)

Brian, was able to get the ball rolling, then she could be right. They could be in their new three-bedroom house in Hannigan Field in time to host a family Christmas there.

Megan was already beginning to brainstorm the next set of matchmaking events before the first snowfall. So far, she had *Faith in the Field*, a mixer for religious types and *Families in the Field*, one for those who hadn't always been single.

In the back of her mind, she wondered if she was straying a little from her brand, though—which was more about *come one, come all.*

That's why she was tentatively planning *Fall in Love in the Field*—cliché. And *Flirt in the Field*—a little sappy, but...

Sarah pulled her dark hair forward and cinched her jeans. "At least there's no uniform."

"And at least you already have a couple of friends there, remember," Megan pointed out.

Over the course of the summer, Sarah had ingratiated herself with two upperclassmen who had already set the stage for a seamless introduction for the pretty new girl. And then there were Mercy and Viviana. The former being Clara's teacher's pet the year before and the latter being Matt Fiorillo's daughter. If ever a new kid had the chance to enter immediate popular status, Sarah had that chance. The only question was whether or not she even wanted it.

More and more, as Sarah grew older, she grew moodier, broodier, and quirkier. Yes, she had gone to every single beach party she could possibly sneak away to. But as much as she had already started to fit in with Birch Harbor teens, she was also compelled to spend lots of time with her Aunt Amelia. If Kate was the leader and Clara the goody-two-shoes and Megan the dark horse, Amelia was the wild spirit of the adult women in Sarah's life.

Of course, Sarah had stayed most of the summer with

Amelia, and it only made sense that they grew close. Still, Megan sometimes worried if moving back to Birch Harbor on a whim wasn't the best decision for her daughter.

Then, she was reminded of how wonderful it was for Sarah to spend more time among her family, and she shook the worry.

"Besides," Megan went on, smoothing the shoulders of her daughter's t-shirt, "Your *aunt* works there."

"Cousin," Sarah corrected her pointedly.

CHAPTER 5—CLARA

"Viviana Fiorillo?" Clara called, glancing over her computer at the neat rows of freshmen, most of them nervous. Some of them prematurely ornery.

Clara settled her warm gaze on the familiar face that matched the name, but the girl was nonplussed. "It's Vivi," she corrected.

Clara's gut clenched, and her eyes darted to the clock. Forty-five minutes until passing period. She blinked and smiled. "Vivi, of course. I know."

In reply, the girl smiled back—her glossy lips stretching across brilliant, straight, white teeth. Swallowing, Clara returned the smile. Everything about Vivi was a version of Clara—an extreme version, as if Clara was cranked through a doll machine. Where Clara's hair was bright blonde, Vivi's was *white* blonde. Where Clara had warm, smooth skin, Vivi's was deep, island tan. And so on and so forth.

"Mercy Hennings," Clara continued, flicking her gaze to the girl in the seat behind Vivi. They shared an easy smile, a knowing one. Mercy raised her hand and nodded.

And on it went, until Clara was through the roster and

learned that she already knew over half the class from the previous school year. The other half—those from St. Mary's or out of town or who had been homeschooled—were by and large quiet. The ones who had already had Clara were compliant if comfortable.

She opened their first day lesson with a simple assignment. An ice-breaker. Each student was to write a short story about himself or herself. It could be fictional in that maybe the *budding writers* (as Clara called them) would cast magical creatures to represent their friends and family. They could pick new names and fantastical events. "But in the end," Clara went on to explain, stepping languidly around her podium and settling half her weight on an empty front desk, "We should learn something about you from your piece of writing."

In typical honors-student fashion, four hands shot up immediately.

Clara called on each in turn.

"How long does it have to be?" one boy asked.

Clara lifted her palms. "As long as it needs to be to satisfy the goal, but you only have thirty minutes." She nodded toward the clock that hung next to the American flag.

A girl asked, "Do we skip lines?"

"Please do." Easier to mark up that way.

Another: "Can I write in pencil?"

"Pen only. Cross through your errors and rewrite in the extra space."

Finally, Clara called on Mercy, the last one with her hand up. "Miss Hannigan," Mercy began. Clara smiled. "Will we have to share out loud?"

In fact, in her lesson plans, Clara had slotted five to ten minutes to allow for one or two students to read aloud if they liked, and so she cocked her head toward the clock again. "If we have time, I'll take a couple of volunteers who'd like to read their pieces. But, no, Mercy. You won't be required to share. These can be personal."

Mercy's face regained color, and she settled into her seat, but the question reminded Clara of something she had learned at the back-to-school in-service for teachers.

"One more thing before you begin, everyone." Her eyebrows fell more heavily and her face solemn. She made eye contact with a few of the unfamiliar students and another few of the familiar ones who she suspected might need to hear what she had to say. "Keep in mind that while I would be honored to be your confidant, if what you share is... well, if it's *serious*, I am a mandated reporter."

Vivi lifted her hand in front of her chest, and Clara couldn't tell if she was raising it. "Vivi? Do you have a question?"

"What do you mean you're a mandated reporter? What do you report?"

The other students sat, rapt, and it occurred to Clara that she ought to be much, much clearer. The first day wasn't ideal to wade into such weedy waters, but for open-ended, *personal* writing assignments, it was critical that students knew their boundaries... and their opportunities. They were encouraged to report abuse, but they were discouraged from penning a tall tale about drinking in the woods or smoking behind the school.

Clara swallowed and considered her next words carefully. "All right," she started, finding her footing, "I'll be frank. If you write a story about drugs or parties, I can't ignore that."

She bit her lip, wondering if her phrasing was off-putting. The students just stared at her.

She went on, "If you write that you're being hurt—by a parent or even another student, I'll report that, too. For your sake," Clara added. After a beat, she continued, "Mandatory reporting means that if I learn a secret about you or your friend, and that secret suggests that you're in trouble— maybe you're dating someone too old or maybe another student corners you in the locker room—I'll help you. That's what it means. So, if you feel like this writing assignment is a good place for you to share about it—if you *or a friend of yours* needs help, then please do. I *will help you.* But if you want to go sneak off to some party next weekend and think it might be funny or cool to write about that, think twice—both about *going* to that party and about *writing* about the party."

When she finished, Clara glanced around the room. She was met mostly with blank faces. This made sense. In an honors class, Clara expected that the kids weren't much for parties, for one, and for two, they generally came from nuclear families, good homes. They didn't need help. They likely wouldn't submit a misguided *cry* for help, either.

But you never knew. That was the thing about teenagers. They surely couldn't be trusted with their own emotions.

All Clara could hope for was to be a confidant and that her students wouldn't abuse that and make a mountain of a molehill.

Her memory returned to her training where the speaker gave an example of how one student wrote a journal entry about a father who mistreated his children. The whole thing turned into an overblown investigation. The dad ended up fired from his job and on the brink of losing custody... and then the child explained it was a fictional story. The line between fiction and reality was blurred, and the teacher had mishandled the whole thing.

Clara offered a kind smile. "Simply this, guys, if you need something, you're welcome to write about it, and you can trust that I'll take that information and do the best I can. But don't get too carried away with storytelling. Keep it school appropriate. And have fun! This is meant to be a fun story about you. Nothing more. Nothing less." She turned her head to Vivi. "Does that answer your question?"

But the girl was already furiously scratching out lines on her paper—unleashed by the assignment.

With only twenty-five minutes left, Clara left the class to work, took a seat behind her desk, and copied names from her computer screen into her hardcopy attendance book. She preferred working with a pencil and paper over a mouse and screen, which perhaps set her apart from other teachers her age. It felt safer, though, to have the physical record of who was in her room during what hour and what they ought to be doing.

Her second period was another Honors English 9 group. After lunch, she'd have two regular English sections. After school, Clara expected to stay and prepare for the next day, but she also felt the need for a celebratory dinner. Or perhaps just appetizers. Maybe even a sip of wine.

In all her years of teaching, Clara had never been one of *those* teachers. The ones who met for happy hour at least once a week. Margarita Mondays or Taco Tuesdays. But with the rush of a new teaching appointment and her own personal changes, it might be nice to have someone to gush to. Especially since her date with Jake was only days away.

Fighting the urge to slide her phone out and text her sisters, she put together a to-do list instead.

Tackle Mom's bedroom. Start on the basement. Fall flowers. New wreath.

Though she didn't have many neighbors up at the

cottage, she had recently taken notice that she wasn't the only one who lived along Birch Creek. How that had escaped her for so many years was beyond Clara. She supposed that she simply didn't spend enough time outdoors. Didn't walk quite far enough to see where in Birch Harbor she was situated.

But in the past couple of weeks, Clara had ventured once along Birch Creek, stumbling past the stretch that she'd previously considered the end. In fact, the end of the creek wasn't where she thought—not where the water disappeared into a smattering of mossy rocks. Instead, it was a buried waterfall, of sorts, where the creek fell down a craggy enclave and streamed beneath black iron bars into Birch Harbor's only gated community: Birch Harbor Heights.

Clara knew precious little about Birch Harbor Heights other than the fact that it was where many of Nora's country club friends lived.

She didn't realize the community backed to the expanse of woods that spanned the nether regions of the cottage.

This proximity to such beautiful homes had elevated Clara and one day, she drove herself to the front and found the gumption to ask the security guard if she could drive through. She didn't give him a good cause. No, she wasn't visiting a friend. No, she wasn't house hunting. She lived on the other side of the gate—in the cottage by the creek. Did he know it? —and would like to see what she couldn't see from her own plot of land.

Surprisingly, the guard let her in, and Clara had the thrill of gawking at beautiful suburban-style homes—each one sitting at the arch of a pretty patterned brick drive with flowers aplenty and green grass for days. Luscious wreaths filled the doors, and pops of color screamed inspiration at her.

So, that's what Clara mentally set about doing: pulling a little of the upper class to her home. She could emulate them. It would give her a goal to aim for and something to distract her when it came time to sort through Nora's personal effects.

She glanced at the clock, then jolted. "Oh, time's up!" Clara chirped, standing and smoothing her floral print dress. She rounded the corner of her desk and returned to her position at the podium, watching as most of the class scrambled to tie up the loose ends in their impromptu life stories. Their miniature historical fictions, as Clara called the assignment in her own mind.

"We have just enough time for one of you to share, if anyone wants?" She started to go on, assuming they'd prefer to be released promptly with the bell. "If not, then go ahead and pass your papers—"

"I'd like to share, Miss Hannigan," came a voice from the center of the room. Viviana's. Vivi's, rather.

"Oh, terrific," Clara replied. "Go right ahead, Vivi. You can read from your desk."

Without hesitation, Vivi sprung up, her paper in her hands. Clara caught sight of the girl's French manicure, and a pang of envy hit her. Clara had never been one for French manicures or false eyelashes, but now here she was: confronted with a longing for some lifestyle far outside of Clara's own. She couldn't help but wonder what kind of father Matt Fiorillo was. How he'd brought up such a feminine, ethereal child as Viviana.

Like an old pro, Vivi cleared her throat and launched into an impeccably clear reading of her one-page story.

"Once upon a time, there was a girl who had a perfect life. She had a loving mother and nice father. Or so she thought." Vivi glanced up ominously. "This girl was beautiful and smart, and her parents always told her she was the most special girl in the whole wide world. Then one day, her mother and father had a serious argument. The girl's mother decided to move far away, to a *better* place, and she wanted to take Viv—" Vivi flushed and cleared her throat again. "Sorry. The mother wanted to take the girl with her to a really spectacular big city, but the father didn't like that. The two parents decided to share their perfect girl—the father kept her over the summer, and the mother kept her over the school year, and life returned to normal. Then one day, when the girl was still very young, the mother and father had another serious argument. They seemed mad at the girl, and so they agreed she would attend a private school instead of a public school." Vivi lifted her eyebrow around the room.

Clara frowned then glanced at the other students, curious about where Vivi was going and if the others were prepared for such a journey. They sat entranced in the bizarre and naked tale of this beautiful newcomer, and so too was Clara. With three minutes left, she nodded at Vivi to go on.

"Soon enough, life returned to being perfect for this little girl. She had lots of friends in her private school, and she spent lots of time on the beach, playing with her friends and enjoying her perfect life. Her father was nice again, and the girl thought she was still the most special thing in the whole world. But all of her life, something was missing for the girl. It wasn't her parents' marriage. It was something else. She realized she didn't like being the most special girl in the whole world. She knew life could be better if she had a best friend."

Clara swallowed. Never in her experience had a four-teen-year-old written and then spoken with such... compulsion. Eeriness, even. With one minute left, she nodded again at Vivi, praying the raw story wasn't some shocking revelation or drawn-out teenage drama.

"Then one summer, life did become better. The girl met another special girl." Vivi twisted and smiled down at Mercy, and Clara released the breath she'd been holding.

"And they became best friends forever."

Clara raised her hands in a quick and quiet applause. The other students suppressed their groans and packed in a fervor, leaving without being dismissed.

Even Mercy, who'd just been at the receiving end of the most enigmatic freshman's affections, anxiously packed and urged her *best friend forever* toward the door.

But Vivi loitered.

With precious time to use the restroom and prepare for the next class, Clara tried to prod her along. "Wonderful story, Vivi. It read a bit like a fairytale, you know. I felt I learned a little of your life, but it didn't come across as a dry autobiography." She began to walk to the classroom door, holding her arm out.

"There's more to it, of course," Vivi answered, strolling slowly to the door behind Mercy, who grew more panicked to waste precious passing time.

Clara grew rigid. "Everyone's life is a complicated story," she answered, placating the child.

Vivi smiled and shrugged. "Maybe I'll write more of mine."

"You do that, Viviana," Clara answered, her gaze narrowing and her desire to escape to the faculty lounge dissipating entirely. "But you'd better hurry to your next class. You wouldn't want to get in trouble."

CHAPTER 6—KATE

"How was your first week back?" Kate asked Clara between sips of her Arnold Palmer.

They sat on the back deck of the Inn—Kate, Amelia, Megan, and Clara—each with a cool drink in hand. A freshly prepared charcuterie board with cheese and crackers and hummus and pita bread sat untouched in the center. The temperature dipped with the sun, and Kate felt rejuvenated.

She'd spent the day with Matt, working on the attic. They came across little of historic value up there, but the few pieces Nora left weren't valueless. Soon, the attic space would become two more guest rooms, and she would be well on her way to financial stability, so long as tourism in Birch Harbor held fast.

She thought it would.

Now, all three of her sisters had arrived for a last-minute at-home happy hour. Their cause for celebration? A new season. Back to school for Clara. A new event to plan for Megan. Amelia's preparations for her grand opening. Kate having Matt all to herself to canoodle and continue work on expanding the Inn. Some days, of course.

Mostly, Matt was busy with his own projects. In fact, he was out at Hannigan Field with Megan's husband Brian, as they spoke. Matt wasn't a home builder or a contractor, but he could help with some of the plans and work, and he wanted to. Brian hired him immediately, and their friendship was fast and easy. It melted Kate's heart.

Clara let out a long breath. "Something funny happened during first period today," she confessed, her brow wrinkling. "Actually, first period has been weird all week." Clara glanced up and met Kate's gaze.

The youngest of the four had been out of the picture all week. She'd gone home each night after school—tired, according to her text messages. Now, it was Friday, and the poor thing looked completely wiped out.

"That's the hour Vivi has you, right? First period?"

Clara nodded at Kate. "She and Mercy Hennings are in there together."

Kate's stomach clenched involuntarily. "So... how is she?"

"Viviana, you mean?" Clara's eyes slid to the platter of finger foods, and she stole a cube of cheese.

"Well, yeah."

"You know I can't technically talk about my students," Clara answered, munching and staring across the backyard toward the lake.

Megan snorted. "Oh come *on*, Clar. You brought it up. Besides, what's the point of having a sister work at the school if we aren't going to get in the insider gossip?"

"Insider gossip?" Amelia chimed in. "That won't come from the school. That'll come from the beach parties those crazy kids flock to in droves. I'm the one with the insider gossip, you know."

"Oh, you are?" Megan asked.

Kate cut in, "Let's be real. Teenagers spend most of their waking hours inside the four walls of Birch Harbor High. And anyway," she glanced meaningfully at Clara, "I don't want *gossip*; I just want to check in."

"I want to hear more about what Amelia has to say regarding the beach parties," Megan protested.

Amelia threw up her hands. "Well, nothing that pertains to your precious Sarah, if that's what you're asking. I'm just talking about how they seem to wander all the way down to the lighthouse from the Village or the southern cove. It's a long walk for a—"

"Floating beach party," Clara quipped. "Happens every weekend. That's the one thing I learned this week. In the teacher's lounge. It's like the number one topic of conversation. You'd be amazed how... *immersed* teachers are in the social lives of their students. I mean, I guess it was sort of like that at the middle school, but the stakes are higher now, you know?"

"So, what kind of a student is Vivi? Come on, Clar, you can tell me. I won't go running to Matt. I promise." Kate clasped her hands in pleading supplication.

"Okay, all right," Clara replied. "But I'm not talking about school as a teacher right now. I'm talking about my job as your *sister*," she answered, grinning a little. Kate smiled back. They hadn't officially agreed on keeping their sister status intact in the wake of the truth, but it seemed that's how Clara wanted to proceed—with Kate as her big sister, just like always.

It made sense. Nora was Clara's mother. Nora raised

Clara. Nora *wanted* Clara for a daughter. Kate knew this to be true, even if it seemed a little wonky.

And Kate could tell another thing, too. As long as she was Clara's sister, then Clara didn't have to come to terms with the matter of Matt Fiorillo.

But if she ever wanted to, then Kate was ready. She'd made it clear in the past, and she'd continue to gently insert the offer where appropriate.

Now wasn't appropriate, though.

Now, Clara just wanted to relax with a drink on a Friday night on the lip of Lake Huron. With her sisters.

And Kate couldn't be happier.

"Well," Clara began, "Viviana is very smart. I mean... *really* smart. Scary smart. She gives Mercy a run for her money."

"Do you think that's the private school influence?" Amelia asked, only half as interested in their conversation as she was, apparently, in the hummus and pita bread. But it was a useful question.

Clara shrugged. "I'm not sure. I'm telling you, though. That girl is just plain whip smart. But I can't get a read on her. Some days, I think she's taunting me. Other days, I think she adores me."

Kate leaned back in her chair. "You know what? I feel the exact same way. Sometimes, she swings by here, randomly. She'll play nice and sweet, and then I'll see her in town the next afternoon, and she ignores me. She's hot and cold."

"Is Matt that way?" Clara asked. "Hot and cold?"

Kate shook her head. "Not at all. He's... even keeled. Consistent."

"What about her mother?"

The question belonged to Megan, which was logical. When it came to family dynamics, Megan always went back to the mom-and-dad factor. It was the matchmaker in her, maybe. Or the deep need to pair people off and break them down—looking at how they functioned. How they ticked.

This time, Kate just blinked. "I don't know much about her—Vivi's mom, I mean. I know she was the type to sort of... give up her daughter." As the words slid out of her mouth, her stomach cramped, and she grew lightheaded. She dropped her chin to her chest. "I can't judge that, I guess."

Amelia squeezed her hand. "No one is judging anything here, Kate," she whispered. But Kate didn't lift her head to meet Clara's gaze.

So, when Clara spoke, Kate's heart raced in her chest.

"Kate, what happened to you was a different matter. You don't need to feel ashamed, okay? I don't. Really, I don't," Clara said.

Kate looked up at last and met her gaze. She never meant for the conversation to turn so heavy, but maybe it was inevitable. Nodding and smiling, she sucked down the threat of tears. "Thanks, Clar. I didn't mean that Vivi's mom is a... a bad mom, either. I don't know her, like I said."

"Does Vivi know her?" Amelia asked pointedly.

Clara answered for Kate. "Yes. According to her, her parents didn't split until she was at least old enough to recall it. And Vivi lived with her mother for a while, too. It was more recently that she moved to Heirloom."

Kate was ready to re-enter the conversation and accept that the secret about Clara could (for now) be water under the bridge. She cleared her throat. "Vivi is closer with Matt. She and her mom butted heads, I think. But everything is better for her here. She's happy."

Nodding, Clara replied, "Good. Maybe I'm being sensitive. It's hard, you know, starting fresh at a new school. For teachers, too."

"For teachers, for freshmen, *and* for seniors," Megan pointed out. "I think Sarah is eating her lunch in the bathroom."

"What?" Kate nearly choked on her drink. "How can that be? She's practically the teen queen of Birch Harbor, and she just moved here."

Megan shook her head. "She said Paige and Chloe have the opposite lunch block. Mercy and Vivi have the same one as Sarah, though. But when she's in the cafeteria, the younger two try to sit with her, and it..." Megan's eyes flashed up. "It embarrasses her, I guess."

Kate swallowed. "Aw, well, that makes sense. They want to take advantage of their cool older friend. And Sarah can't compromise her reputation to play big sister to freshmen."

Megan shrugged. "I don't know. I think she needs an extracurricular."

"Drama," Amelia answered.

Kate huffed. "It's all drama at that age."

"No," Amelia replied. "I mean *drama*."

CHAPTER 7—CLARA

The following day, Clara couldn't eat a thing. Her plans with Jake had been a distraction all week, but now she needed a distraction from him.

By noon, and with nothing good enough to wear, she called Amelia.

"Help," Clara whined into the phone.

"What? Are you cleaning the basement again?" Amelia's voice took on an exasperated effect.

"No, I mean for my date. I feel sick, Am. Literally sick. I'm shaking, and I have no clue what I'll wear, and—"

"Okay, first of all, you should eat something *now*. You don't want to faint."

Clara frowned. "I *can't*. I'm frozen over here."

"Well, come to the lighthouse, then. I'll put you to work here. I have lots you and Sarah can do."

"Is Sarah there?" Clara asked.

"Yep. She's trying to format my brochure."

"You're making brochures already?"

"I want to open on Saturday, October third. But Michael

thinks we should delay a month. Too much going on. His work. The case..."

"You're not talking about—"

"Dad," Amelia replied. "It's not over, you know, Clar."

To Clara, the case of the missing Wendell Acton was a nonstarter. She'd never met the man, and from her tinted view, he was nothing more than a deadbeat. Worse than Matt, even. Maybe much worse, if Matt was telling the truth about hoping to be a part of Clara's life.

"OKAY, so you two can keep at it with content and formatting. Sarah, don't forget to reference my notes." Amelia slid a page full of chicken scratch closer to the computer. "We also need bulk printing. I'm talking to my friends from the Players to see if they'd be interested in staging a historical re-enactment for the opening and—"

"When is the opening, again?" Clara interrupted as she lowered herself next to Sarah at the kitchen table.

"I told you, I'm aiming for October third."

"So, you're going to have an event on that day, too? Like Kate with the Inn?"

"Yes, that's the plan. We've got to draw attention. So anyway, if they can pull something off in a couple of weeks, and if Michael can get all the paperwork filed in time, then October third is *totally* doable."

"What day of the week is that?" Sarah asked.

"Saturday," Clara and Amelia replied in tandem.

"That's Homecoming, then. You'll lose out on anyone going to Homecoming, you know."

Amelia and Clara exchanged a small smile.

"Well, cheerleaders and the local marching band aren't

exactly my target demographic," Amelia began. Clara shot her a look, and Amelia added, "But you're right." She let out a sigh.

"Maybe you should take Michael's advice and hold off for a few more weeks." Clara began reading over Sarah's shoulder, starting with the Hannigan and Acton family histories on the left side of the screen and sweeping down to an introduction of the museum director and curator, *Amelia Ann Hannigan.*

Her older sister answered, "What if it's too cold, though? Halloween is, like, the breaking point between fall and winter. And you know there's nothing worse than going to an outdoor event when it's cold. Trust me. I've been to one too many winter weddings."

"But you're having it in the daytime, right?" Clara asked.

"Yes, but it might be cold in the daytime, too. Keep in mind the visitors will be standing around, not going for a midday jog." Amelia hesitated. "I'll look up the weather, and we'll go from there."

Sarah explained what she'd done so far while Amelia took her phone out and thumbed her way online.

"So, Aunt Clar—or, I mean *Clara*,"

"You can still call me Aunt, you know," Clara replied, her eyes moving across to the center section of the online pamphlet. *Lighthouses on Lake Huron,* it read.

"It's a little awkward either way," Sarah confessed. "I'll just… well, anyway, Aunt Amelia wants a page of attractions, a page of events, and a page of resources. She gets extra funding if we can pull in sponsors, too, whatever that means. So, we need to add multiple pages, but I'm not sure what should go after the lighthouse overview." Sarah pointed at the center of the screen.

"Hmm." Clara drummed her fingers on the table, her

eyes drifting down the neatly laid-out document on the laptop. "Let's move hours of operation and location to the back page. Do you have a back page yet?"

Sarah clicked twice, and it appeared, complete with a lighthouse logo and the newly minted name that Amelia had registered: *The Birch Harbor Lighthouse and Museum*. It lacked originality, but perhaps that wasn't a bad thing when it came to business branding.

Clara directed Sarah back to the first section. "You're good at this, you know. Graphic design, I suppose you'd call it?"

"I took a class back home. It's easy, though. Just takes a little time." She typed from Amelia's handwritten notes.

"Do you think that's what you'd like to do after you graduate? Study graphic design?"

Sarah shook her head. "No way. I'm all about the water. I want to be a marine biologist. In California or Florida or somewhere."

"Really?" Clara asked. "You know Mercy's dad is a marine biologist. Or *was*. He taught at college, but he spent a lot of time on the Great Lakes. Fresh water research or something." Clara stopped herself. "At least, that's what Mercy told me."

Sarah's eyebrow picked up. "I didn't know he taught college kids. That's pretty cool. But now he's just a marina manager." She shrugged.

Clara leaned back. "*Just* a marina manager? He heads up Birch Harbor Marina. It's a huge job, you know."

"I didn't mean anything. I just... I don't know. Why would you do that if you were a biologist? You know? Sounds like a... downgrade."

"I think he wanted to spend more time on the water rather than writing about it, maybe." Clara didn't really know *why* Jake Hennings gave up a great job to move to the lake and deal with tourists, actually. It was her own romantic assumption she shared with Sarah, privately. She stowed the question for their date that night, feeling suddenly more comfortable. Less jittery. "Are there any snack foods around here?"

Sarah pointed to the kitchen counter. "Apples for days."

Clara rose and grabbed one. Then a second. Then she popped open the cupboard and took out a glass for water and filled it, chugging like a frat boy until the whole glass had disappeared.

She let out a sigh. "I feel a little better now."

Sarah giggled. "I didn't know that adults got nervous for dates."

Clara grinned at her. "We're human, too."

Amelia broke into their conversation. "Okay, so the temps totally drop off at the end of October. There is no way I can open with food trucks and the re-enactment in *November*. It *has* to be earlier. October tenth. That's the latest we can do it and still maintain some degree of comfort." She was talking a mile a minute. "No pun intended."

Clara cut in, "I don't want you to get sensitive, Am, but how in the world are you going to sustain this through the winter if you're worried about late October? I mean, it's going to get a lot colder. Will you still have... *patrons*? Or whatever you call them?"

Amelia gave her a look. "Obviously, business will dwindle in the colder months because tourism dwindles. But I've got great ideas. First," she went on, grabbing an apple for herself and polishing it on her shirt like a cartoon character, "the lighthouse will remain open year round as a museum. It costs little to keep it going, and I'll nab the weekend warriors and weekday seniors who are looking for something to do. Secondly, I reached out to the county artists' association. I offered to act as an on-location gallery at a low rate. They're *interested*, Clara." Amelia rounded the table and pulled a chair too close, her eyes ablaze. "And that's not *all*, either. I'm going to partner with Megan and rent out the lighthouse for date nights."

"Date nights? You're going to charge Megan for her matchmaking clients to come to the lighthouse?" Clara frowned.

"No, no, no. It'll be wrapped up in their fee. Megan is going to give me a cut of profits in exchange for getting first dibs on reservations after eight o'clock at night."

"It sounds like—"

"But wait, there's *more*," Amelia continued, jabbing a finger at the screen. Sarah scrolled for her, apparently in on the various hustles and schemes that Amelia had thought up.

Clara's eyes focused. "Murder Mystery Dinner Theatre?" She frowned. "Amelia, have you gone *mad*?"

Amelia grinned. "We all go a little mad sometimes, you know." Then she shook her head. "But seriously, it's perfect. I'll book small parties and host a dinner and enlist the Players to trickle along in the group for a night of perfect fall fun."

"A night of perfect fall fun," Clara echoed, growing adrift with overwhelm. "You're planning all of that, *and* you're still looking for Wendell?" Clara never knew which term to use for him. Dad? Wendell? *Your* dad, when talking to her sisters?

This was becoming a running theme in the family—who had earned which title and how—and Clara didn't like it.

Sarah pushed away from the laptop. "I think it all sounds like a lot of fun," she snapped defensively.

"I don't mean to be *critical*, but come on, you two. You've got a lot on your plates. And Sarah, you've got school to think of. And your new friends, right?" She knew she sounded like a big fat guilt trip crashing a party of two, but wasn't it her duty to shed a little reality on the situation?

Sarah slapped the computer shut. "I'm taking a break. I'll be on the dock."

"Isn't there a beach party tonight?" Clara called after her. "I heard about it from the other teachers."

"I'm not going!" Sarah answered over her shoulder as she left the house.

Clara felt Amelia's eyes burning on her. "We're busting our butts here, Clar. Sarah's excited for all of this, you know? And it's good for her."

"Good for her? Amelia," Clara argued. "I know you mean well. But can't you see that Sarah needs to assimilate at school? Megan was just talking about this last night. If she's too wrapped up with you, she'll keep... I don't know. She'll keep eating lunch in the bathroom or something. You need to cut her loose a little."

Amelia let out a long breath. "I don't know if I agree, Clar. I mean, I think that if she wants to be here helping me, then she should be able to. It's safer anyway, right?"

"Safer than what?" Clara asked. "Safer than having no one to turn to at school? No one to talk to on the phone at night like you and your girlfriends used to do? Jamming up the line and sending Mom into a conniption fit?"

They shared a small smile, and Clara went on, "Am, I know what it's like to have no friends at school. I know what it's like to give up your childhood for an adult. I did it. Trust me. I mean, yeah. You're way... *cooler* than Mom. You're younger and fun, and Sarah's probably having fun, that's true. But if you keep assigning her tasks, then she'll grow further away from those kids who first took an interest."

Amelia's gaze narrowed. "I get what you mean, Clara, but I don't think it's a *bad* idea to distract her from those crazy beach parties. Right? I mean, I went to my fair share of them, so I know exactly what I'm talking about here." She shook her head. "Anyway, Clara, you and Sarah are nothing alike. Sarah is naturally social. She makes friends easily, and she fits in. But if she finds her niche outside of Birch Harbor High, then that's okay, too."

Clara shook her head, confused. "What do you mean 'we're nothing alike?' What are you saying?"

"I'm saying to let her do what she wants to do."

"No, what are you saying about *me*?" Clara asked, her eyes stinging.

Amelia balked. "*Nothing*, oh my gosh, Clar." She pressed her hand to her head and massaged it. "Okay, I'm sorry. I guess... I guess I'm saying that you put a lot of focus on school. And then you never stopped. You went to college, then you went right back to school—to become a teacher. And you did all that despite the fact that you never were much for things like homecoming or sports or choir. You worked at school, you went home and worked, you went back to school and started all over again."

"And that's exactly what you're doing with Sarah. Dragging her in on the weekends to help you cobble together some wild notion of professional success." Clara shook her head. "All I'm saying is to encourage Sarah to have a normal senior year. Megan would appreciate it, if nothing else."

"No way," Amelia answered. "She's going to have more than a normal, average senior year here. She's going to have an amazing one. And I'm going to see to it."

Clara's nostrils flared. How could her older sister still be so immature?

Then again, was there something to be said for Amelia's approach? Was there something to be said for bonding with a younger girl and shaping her into the person she wanted to be? Rather than pushing her away?

Clara had no clue.

And maybe that was the problem. All she knew was a life of directions. Rules. Studying and reading and passing that on to the next generation.

"Just promise me one thing, Am," she said at last, exasperated with the argument.

"What's that?"

"Promise me you'll leave her out of the Wendell thing. Okay?"

Amelia's face remained flat. "Fine."

"Really?" Clara's eyes lit up. She'd made headway.

"Yeah. I don't have time for it anyway. It's Michael's focus now. And it's dead. The whole case. I mean, as much as I'm desperate to know what happened, I don't think we'll ever get an answer."

It was coming too quickly. Too easily. Amelia was too ready to give in. Clara's spine prickled in suspicion. "One more thing, actually. The whole yearbook discovery with Mom and Judith. You'll let that go, too?"

"Why should I?" Amelia returned, her cheeks growing red.

"It's the same problem as Wendell. A dead end. And it's pointless, Am," Clara said. "I just think you need a little focus, okay? And if you're doing all this crazy stuff with your business *and* researching Wendell *and* researching Judith The Snake Carmichael... well, I worry you won't be able to pull it off."

Amelia crossed her arms over her chest. "You know what?"

Clara frowned. "What?"

"I'm more worried about *you*." Amelia uncrossed her arms and stabbed a finger at Clara.

"What are you talking about?" Clara's life was going great. New job. New house. New year...

"I'm worried that you have a date in a few hours, and you're *here*, nagging us." A grin flickered along Amelia's lips. "Come on. We're going shopping."

Clara let her hands drop to her sides. Reasoning with Amelia was useless, but her sister wasn't wrong. Clara's priorities were perhaps a little misdirected. Her emotions, too.

She could use a little fun. They all could.

"Let's grab Sarah and get out of here. I mean I talked to Sherryl, our stage manager, and she's already going to set about hiring a writer. So, my wild ideas can wait. Your love connection cannot."

Following Amelia out of the house, Clara lifted her hand to shield her eyes from the midday sun as she searched the beach for Sarah.

"Sarah!" Amelia called.

There was no sight of her.

Glancing back to Clara, Amelia called out again, louder. "*Sarah!*"

Still nothing. Fresh panic rose in Clara's chest, and she began to jog toward the water line.

But as soon as she passed the lighthouse, she saw her, sitting in the sand just north of the dock, perfectly out of sight.

"Sarah!" Clara cried over the throb of waves and the

squawks of lake gulls. "You scared us, we couldn't see you, and we—"

Sarah stood up, brushed sand from her butt, and pointed.

Clara followed her finger out to the water. "What?" she asked.

Amelia came up behind them both, squinting into the lapping whitecaps as a speedboat chugged across their eyeline. A whipping wind threw her hair across her face, hiding her reaction.

"Marine Patrol," Sarah replied.

Clara dropped her hand. "Oh, yeah. So what?"

"I didn't know there were, like, *lake* police or whatever."

Amelia bent over and grabbed Sarah's hand. "Who cares about that? Clara and I have an errand to run, and *you* have a beach party to get ready for."

CHAPTER 8—AMELIA

They'd found something at White Birch Boutique in the Village. A coral dress with pretty lace cap sleeves. It hit just above Clara's knees, and Amelia herself nearly swooned.

After finalizing the sale and a lazy lunch, all three returned to the cottage. Jake was picking Clara up at five—early dinner and then an evening boat ride.

Clara popped into the shower, leaving Amelia and Sarah to roam the cottage.

"Does she really need us to stick around?" Sarah whined. "I was almost done with the pamphlet. I could still finish if we head back now."

Amelia rummaged in the cupboard for a snack—she'd eaten only a salad at lunch. It left her hungry, as usual. "She might need help with hair and makeup, so yes, we do need to stick around. At least, *I'm* sticking around. No way will I miss Clara's first big date. But if you want to go back, I can call Michael to give you a ride."

Michael's Saturdays had grown into a point of contention, truth be told. At the very start of their relationship (which was still new, of course), he and Amelia took daytrips together, toured the limits of Birch Harbor, and explored beyond into the suburbs and nearby towns. Those weekends settled into cozy nights at the lighthouse or at Michael's house in Harbor Hills—a place he'd deemed too big and too fancy for a single man.

Amelia had reminded him he wasn't single, and he reminded her that, legally, he was.

Oddly, it was one of the most romantic things he had ever said to her—the implication hung like a promising rain cloud after forty days of drought, and Amelia clung to it.

But since then, Saturdays became something else altogether. If Michael wasn't helping at the lighthouse, he was researching Wendell's case. If he wasn't researching Wendell's case, Amelia hinted that he might join up with the other Hannigan women's men at the field to put in a little sweat on that project.

All too soon, Amelia realized that Michael had become something of an errand boy, and it didn't sit well with either one of them. And more recently, Michael's interest in her father's case had turned into something else entirely—like an obsession that was separate from Amelia, almost.

But even with his elbow-deep investigation, he continued to come up empty-handed, finding exactly what police had found in 1992 and the years thereafter: nothing.

And that, Amelia suspected, was part of their disconnect —Michael's impatience with his own inability to help Amelia achieve the one thing she needed.

The thought was sweet, but even Amelia wasn't sure how to handle the dead end. And she didn't understand why their romantic weekends had slowed to a stop.

"No, that's awkward," Sarah answered. "My mom always told me not to ride alone with men."

Amelia's cheeks grew hot, and she frowned. "Oh. Right. I guess that's probably good advice." Though she didn't know where Megan learned it. Nora had certainly never set that tone. Then again, maybe she should have.

Amelia shook the thought, but her chest still felt heavy under the notion that Michael wasn't trustworthy. Or at least, not trustworthy *yet*.

"You know what, Sarah? I'll just drop you home after this. I can finish the brochure, and you need to get ready for the party, right?"

Sarah crossed her arms over her chest, sulking. "Please, come *on*," she whined. "I really don't want to go to that."

"Listen, Clara made a really good point when she and I were talking. She said you need to, you know, be well-rounded. Have friends and all that. And she's right. My girl-friends in high school were the highlight of my life. And my sisters, too. So you need to go, Sarah. The party will be fun. All summer you went to these things. Why are you suddenly disinterested?"

Sarah ignored her and instead pulled her phone from her back pocket.

"What are you doing?" Amelia asked.

"Getting a ride home," Sarah answered, holding the device to her ear and staring at Amelia through a pout. "Mom? Can you come get me from Clara's and take me back to the apartment?"

Sighing, Amelia returned to the cabinet and found a box of crackers. She took it to the counter and munched mind-lessly, studying the place.

In all her time traveling the world in search of a great role or even a good one, she'd missed a lot. She'd missed her mother's decline, there in the cottage. She'd missed Clara's fight to keep some semblance of normality. Suddenly awash with guilt, the crackers crumbling along her dry tongue, she shoved the plastic sleeve back in the box.

Sarah finished her conversation and pushed her phone back in her pocket. "My mom's at the field. She can't get me." Her expression sour, the teenager had moved well beyond the fun they shared browsing for clothes and gossiping over lunch.

Amelia sighed. "I'm going to help Clara get ready. And you have the night off. So, you can either wait with me, or we can call someone else. Maybe Aunt Kate is free."

"The beach party starts at six. If I *have* to go, then I can't just sit around here and wait. I need to get ready, too," Sarah reasoned.

"I'll call Kate," Amelia replied, growing more irritated by the second. Now, all that Clara had said felt even more appropriate, but for a different reason entirely. Amelia had no patience for children, and if her niece was going to act like one... well, then she could spend her weekend holed up at The Bungalows or wafting along the beach with a throbbing crowd of tanned teenagers. Amelia didn't care which.

"Hey," she said to Kate when the call went through. "Are you busy right now?" She flicked a glance to Sarah who had plopped onto the loveseat, her phone glowing on her face.

"WHERE'S SARAH?" Clara asked when she came out of the bathroom ten minutes later.

"Kate picked her up so she could go to the beach party," Amelia answered. "That dress is stunning on you. Have you been laying out or something?" she asked, referring to her little sister's sun-kissed shoulders.

Clara did a spin and grinned. "Fake tanning lotion. I

bought some at the grocery store yesterday. It was on sale." Then she added, "I'm happy for Sarah. She deserves a little fun. What happened, you know? She was hitting every party earlier in the summer."

Nodding, Amelia shrugged. "It's hard being the new girl, even if you're already *in* with the right crowd."

"I wouldn't know. I was never even *in* with the wrong crowd," Clara joked.

Amelia's heart burned for her little sister. With their age difference, it was easy to get lost in all the ways they weren't alike. All the experiences they didn't share—the ones that Amelia had blazed through a decade earlier. But now here she was, faced with the chance to be the big sister she didn't quite get to be when she still lived at home and Clara was just a baby.

"Okay." Amelia rubbed her hands together. "Hair and makeup. I vote less is more, but we can experiment a little."

"Sounds good to me." Clara led her into her bedroom at the far end of the hall. There, she'd set up a small vanity in the corner, complete with a mirror and a wooden box of organized makeup essentials.

"I had no idea you were so prepared," Amelia admired. "And where did you get this table?"

"It was in the basement. I think it must have been Mom's when she was a girl. I don't remember ever seeing it when I was younger, though. Not even in the basement."

Amelia pulled Clara's hair into a series of clips on top of her head. "Well," she replied, "That was Mom for you. Always moving stuff around as if she was looking for a perfect hiding spot. Who knows what in the world she was hiding, though."

"Me, for starters," Clara answered flatly.

Amelia stopped mid-blush application. "What do you mean, 'you?'"

"Well, she sort of kept me hidden away. I mean first when I was born, right? And then the rest of my life. I was always at one of our houses, toiling away."

Swallowing, Amelia continued to work on Clara's face, studying her smooth, clear skin. Her thin lips and small nose—two features that didn't belong to the other Hannigan sisters. "Well," she tried, letting out a sigh, "Mom didn't know what to make of the whole thing. She didn't have anyone other than us, you know? No family. Not even Dad's parents. She had to forge her way into the social scene in town."

"Actually," Clara replied, blinking as Amelia worked a few strokes of mascara into her lashes.

"Don't blink!" Amelia warned.

"Sorry! *Actually*, what I was saying was I sort of had a revelation."

"What do you mean?" Amelia picked up the eyebrow brush and shot a layer of hairspray onto it, sweeping Clara's sparse brows into neat arches.

"When I found out I was Kate's, everything made sense. Mom didn't put me to work so she could go have fun. She put me to work so I couldn't go have fun."

Amelia shook her head. "That wasn't Mom. Trust me."

As Amelia drew a line of waxen highlighter down the center of Clara's nose, Clara grabbed her wrist. "Trust *me*, it was."

Popping the cap back on each pencil and tube, Amelia leaned away. "You look perfect, but you're wrong. Mom was desperate to keep her reputation intact, but not desperate enough to compromise your upbringing. It all goes back to your nature. If even *once* you'd have stood up to her and just said that you were going out, she'd have done nothing. I assure you. Take it from someone who couldn't sit still in the house over on the harbor. We worked, too. Cleaned bathrooms, helped with repairs. But we played."

Clara shook her head. "That's because you were the *we*, Am. I was just the *me*. I didn't have what you had. I only had my chores. And my books."

"And if you wanted to, you could have had friends, Clar. I know Mom wasn't trying to enslave you. Come *on*. You're acting like you're the next iteration of Cinderella." Amelia tried to laugh, but it fell flat.

Maybe Clara wasn't all wrong. Maybe Nora did want to protect her from the same fate as Clara's biological mother and grandmother who didn't know quite how to protect themselves.

Then again, did Kate need protection from Matt? Certainly not. She didn't need protection at all. Clearly.

"You know what?" Amelia pinched open the clips and combed her fingers through Clara's hair. "You could be right, Clar. But it's in the past. Tonight, we celebrate the new you. You're not locked up. You're *unchained*." She wiggled her eyebrows, and Clara couldn't help but giggle.

"Speaking of chains, do I need jewelry?"

"Don't you have some?" Amelia glanced around the vanity.

"Not really. Just silver hoops I never wear."

"What about Mom's? Did you come across any more of her costume jewelry here?"

Clara shook her head, but Amelia was already tugging open the vanity drawers, beginning with the bigger bottom ones and moving up.

"Here, move over," Amelia nudged Clara away from the

center drawer. She pulled from the bottom lip, but it didn't budge.

"It's locked," Clara pointed to the tarnished brass-trimmed keyhole in the center. "I've tried already."

"A locked drawer?" Amelia gasped. "And you didn't tell us?"

CHAPTER 9—MEGAN

She was at the field with Brian and a handful of others—the contractor, his site leader, plus Matt and Michael.

"I think we can call it a day," Megan announced. "Thanks for giving us your Saturday, everyone."

They hadn't broken ground, but the plans were settled, and they were bigger than Megan and Brian initially planned.

It was her sisters who talked Megan into adding a second building on the property—a barn for indoor events. Come winter, she wouldn't regret it. So long as the business brought in a return on the investment, it'd be fine.

Now she could settle her focus on Sarah's new school and final year before college.

But after the long day—and even longer summer—she figured it might be nice to break the ice with her new local friends.

"Are you two up for joining Brian and me for dinner at the Village?" she asked Michael and Matt as they started for the parking lot on the far side of the access road.

"I've gotta go get Vivi and bring her back to town," Matt said.

"What for?" Megan asked.

"She's meeting her friends for a get-together on the beach, I guess."

Sarah hadn't mentioned a get-together. Was she invited? Maybe not. Maybe she was and didn't want to go. Not if it was a freshman thing. Is that part of the reason she'd called Megan for a ride? Hopefully not, otherwise she'd just stood in the way of her daughter's social career. "Is it another school bonfire?"

Matt took a swig from his water bottle and shook his head. "I don't think so. Just kids doing the beach thing." He checked his watch. "Oh, hell. I'm late."

"Why not call Kate?" Brian suggested. "She can take the boat over and bring Viviana back for you, I'm sure."

Megan held up a hand. "It's getting darker earlier, you know," she reasoned. "Maybe it's too late for a beach party?" Not normally one to rain on someone's parade, Megan bit her lip. The suggestion came out awkwardly.

Matt just shrugged. "She'll be with Mercy and a few older girls. Besides, she'll kill me if I change my mind and tell her no."

Glancing out at the shoreline, Megan frowned. Older girls? As in... Sarah? Maybe Sarah did plan to go but didn't even mention it. "Well, Brian's right. You could call Kate. Or even Amelia. She has Sarah with her, after all." Pleased with herself for finding a way to pull Sarah back into the fold, even if not by her daughter's own volition, Megan smiled.

"Oh, perfect." Matt dug his phone from his pocket and put a call through to his girlfriend. "Kate? Hi, how are you?" He nodded and glanced up at Megan. "Good, good. Hey, I have a huge favor to ask. I told Vivi I'd come pick her up and bring her back to the shore for that beach party tonight, but I'm just now leaving the field and—oh? You don't mind? Yes, the keys are in the top drawer of your desk there." He smiled at Megan. "Great, hon. Okay, I'll see you at the Inn." He clicked off and glanced back up. "Ferrying in and out from the Island is a hassle. I'll tell you that. Soon enough, Viv will want her own boat. Mark my words." He chuckled, but Megan's smile faded.

"Sarah doesn't even have her own *car*, let alone a boat," she pointed out. Had life in Birch Harbor changed this drastically? Or had the Stevensons stumbled into a different zip code? When Megan and her sisters were young, no Birch Harbor kids had their own boats. Not even the rich ones. Then again, back then, St. Mary's was less of a factor. If memory served Megan, she recalled only a couple of veritable no-name kids trudging into first period from the Island. Their trek wasn't a flashy one. More like a pilgrimage, really.

Brian came to Vivi's defense, though. "Well, it sounds like Vivi needs a boat more than a car. I mean, do you guys even drive around out on Heirloom? And when you're in town, where do you keep your work truck anyway?"

"I used to keep it at my buddy's house on the southern cove, but now Kate lets me park on the far side of the boathouse. And she lets me keep the boat there, too. But I'll probably go back to the old way. No point in taking up space now that Kate's expanding the Inn."

Megan nodded but then changed the subject back to the so-called get-together. "Well, hopefully Sarah makes it to the beach in time, too. Amelia is notorious for being late." She glanced at her wristwatch, unaware of the start time or any other details. At least Vivi was also delayed. She swallowed and pulled her phone out of her pocket, shooting a text to Amelia.

Michael chuckled. "I can go get Sarah, if you'd like?"

Her phone buzzed instantly.

Amelia.

Kate's on her way to get Sarah for the party. No worries.

Shaking her head, Megan let out a breath, smiled, and thanked him. "Looks like everything is in place."

"In that case, I'm going to head home, actually. I'm wiped out. What a week," Michael answered, offering a handshake each to Brian and Matt.

"Tell me Amelia's not putting you to work on the Wendell thing still," Megan added wryly.

He shook his head. "She's not, but I'm working on it, still. It's interesting to me, you know? I wish my dad were still around. He'd probably know the whole story."

"Really?" Megan asked, her interest piqued.

"Oh yeah. My dad Mr. Matuszewski knew this town in and out. From a distance, though. He was a... quiet observer. Kept a low profile. I wouldn't be surprised if he were friends with your dad, and we just never knew about it." He offered a smile. "Anyway, I've got a different case that needs reading."

"Who's suing who?" Megan pried, unable to help herself. Brian gave her a look, but she just shrugged. "Can't help it. It's the meddler in me."

Michael replied, "It's actually big news around the Island. I can't go into much detail, but it has to do with St. Mary's."

"The *school*?" Megan's eyes grew wide.

He nodded. "Education drama, if there's such a thing." Lowering his voice, Michael added, "Islanders want the administration to reinstate high school grades. There's a hullabaloo about a charter school opening up out there if St. Mary's won't offer grades nine through twelve."

"Wait a minute." Megan's brows knitted together. "Didn't they used to have one?" Megan asked, her memory stirring to life. *That's* why so few kids came into town for school. At one point in time, St. Mary's did offer secondary. Or wait... was that even before Megan was in school? She shook her head, now uncertain. What year was the yearbook Clara had discovered? She hadn't asked, and Amelia had squirreled the thing away as part of her little detective project.

"Yes, but that was before it went co-ed. It used to be a school for girls only. That was a whole other ordeal. If you ask me, the Department of Education should come in and open a public K-12 building. Something small but comprehensive enough to serve the Island kids."

Megan shook her head. "I disagree."

Brian turned to her. "Why? It's crazy those kids have to take a ferry over here for school. Especially the little ones. If they opt out of St. Mary's—that's quite a commute."

"It's what makes us interesting, though," Megan argued.

"*Us*?" Brian asked. "Weren't you always opposed to lumping Heirloom Island in with Birch Harbor?"

She raised and dropped her shoulders. "Well, I still think there's no point in overhauling the educational system. Heirloom Island is technically part of Birch Harbor, and I think it's important to pull those outlying kids into the school system *here*. It would help round out Birch Harbor Unified. You know? Keeps the funding centralized. No competition and a better mix."

"I don't know," Michael interjected. "The history there is too murky for my taste. I think those kids could use a second option that doesn't require braving Lake Huron every morning and afternoon."

"Those kids brave the lake every weekend with these *beach parties*," Megan pointed out.

Brian said, "Either way, as long as the vessel is seaworthy —and the beach isn't too poorly lit—I think it's okay to let them have their little adventures, right?"

"That's true," Matt added. "We sure had ours, after all." He offered a lopsided grin, which made Megan want to sock him in the shoulder on Kate's behalf, but it was hard to be mad at Matt. He was too much of a sweetheart.

"Not a bad point," Michael agreed. "After all, life only seems to get more boring once you grow up. Let them have their teenage dramas, I say."

A shadow crossed the parking lot, and Michael loaded into his truck. Beyond him, Matt waved them off and got into his. Brian and Megan pulled themselves into their SUV, but as they did, Megan's gaze followed the lawyer. He was an enigma to her. Unmarried. Well off. Well connected. Smart. Good looking. Most of all, levelheaded and reasonable. A thought occurred to her.

"Brian?" Megan asked once they were buckled in and on the road. "What do you think Michael sees in Amelia?"

CHAPTER 10—CLARA

Clara shrugged at Amelia. "Why would I call you to say there's a small locked drawer in a beat-up old vanity from the basement?" As the words formed on her tongue, the lightbulb clicked. "Oh," she added. "Right. Well, I'm not currently on a manhunt, so…"

"Aren't you interested in our mother's past? Doesn't something like a *locked drawer* inspire a little curiosity?" Amelia shook her head.

Clara tugged uselessly on it. "I guess I'm more of a *leave the past in the past* kind of person."

Amelia scooped up a bobby pin from the vanity and pinched it between her fingers victoriously.

"Ta-da!" she cheered. "Move aside. Let the pro handle this."

She fiddled for less than a minute, and then they heard a distinct *click*.

Without opening it, Amelia removed the bobby pin and backed away. "Okay. There you go."

Shaking her head, Clara took a step even farther back. "No, this is your mission. Not mine. Whatever is in that drawer, I want nothing to do with it. Jake is picking me up in fifteen minutes, Am."

Amelia glanced at the clock on the bedside dresser and seemed to consider the point.

"There's probably nothing in there," she reasoned aloud.

"What if there is?"

"Then we set it aside and study it later."

Clara's eyes flew to the clock, too. "I really need to get ready, and I'm worried you won't be able to 'set it aside' for later."

"So, you *do* think there's something in there, don't you?" Amelia answered, her eyes blazing.

Turning her attention to the mirror and her wet hair, Clara moved to the vanity and pressed her hips against the drawer. "I have to get ready. My date is more important."

Amelia's face fell. She looked stricken but replied, "I'm sorry, Clara," then took a step forward and pulled a lock of Clara's hair into her hands, twisting it. "You're right. Hair first. Date first. Locked drawers another day."

Clara brightened. "I have an idea. I'll give you the spare key. You can stay here after Jake picks me up. You can go through the drawer and anything else in this place to your heart's content. Deal?"

Amelia grinned. "Deal."

"There's a catch, though," Clara cautioned, assuming the upper hand.

"Oh?"

"You've gotta be gone within two hours."

Amelia frowned. "Is this, like, a *challenge* or something? A gameshow?"

"No." Clara shook her head. "If I bring Jake in for a nightcap, I can't have you here."

Amelia's mouth fell open. "A *nightcap*?" she cried. "Who are you, and what have you done with my baby sister?"

Clara couldn't force away the grin. "I'm not talking about anything *indecent*, but if everything goes well, then I want to be sure we can have the place to ourselves. For a glass of iced tea or wine, even. Okay?"

"Okay," Amelia answered. "But what if you're back in, like, an hour?" she added, her brow line falling.

Clara took her seat again and centered herself in front of the mirror, passing Amelia a round brush. "If I'm back before two hours, that means something went wrong."

WHEN THE DOORBELL RANG, the sisters shrieked like little girls, and Clara shushed Amelia. "Don't come out for ten minutes. Just to be safe."

"I promise," Amelia answered, slapping Clara playfully away. "Now go. Go!"

Clara slipped out of the bedroom, smoothing her coral dress and fiddling with a strand of her blonde hair. It hung light and swishy above her shoulders, and she felt like she might lift up and float to the front door.

She took a deep breath, quelling the nerves pinching in her stomach as she reached for the doorknob and pulled it open.

"*Wow*," Jake breathed the word out, falling back a step. Clara smiled, self-conscious and flattered and thrilled all at once. "You look beautiful," he added.

"Thank you. So do you," she replied, catching herself and slapping her palm on her forehead. "I mean, *handsome*. You look *handsome*." And he did.

Jake Hennings stood in khaki shorts and a light blue

button-down, the sleeves rolled up to his elbows. Long tan limbs and his thick, dirty blonde hair belied his age, which she'd pegged for late thirties, early forties. A bouquet of daffodils and lilies burst from his fist as he offered it to her.

"For you," he added. "I don't know much about flowers, so I asked the woman at the shop to help and—"

"They're beautiful," Clara cut in, taking them and inhaling the sweet scent. No roses, she noted to herself. A smart move for a man in his situation. Safe. "Thank you, Jake." She glanced up at him, using his name and making eye contact, just like she'd read to do. I'll just pop these in a vase, and we can go?"

"Oh, yes. Of course," he answered, following her into the kitchen.

Clara had never been on that sort of a date before. The sort that wasn't preceded by half-hearted texting conversations and profile snooping. Not even in high school or college—especially not then—when dates came on the heels of a late-night study session or with an impromptu, post-class invitation to the Student Union.

She didn't own her *own* vases, even. Never had cause. But, of course, beneath the kitchen sink, she found rows of crystal and glass vases of every size. She handed the bouquet to him before reaching deep into the back of the cupboard.

Carefully removing the biggest one she could spot, she placed it in the sink and turned the tap on until it was three-quarters full. Jake passed back the bouquet, which she inserted and set on the breakfast bar. "That was so kind of you," she said, worrying her fingers together. "Thank you."

They tested out small talk on the way to his car, the door of which he opened for her before jogging around the back to his own side.

A giggle bubbled up in Clara's chest. She felt like she was on a date in a movie, with all the bells and whistles. Every moment was sharp and predetermined. Ritualistic and robotic, even. But that was okay. Clara liked having a sense of what to expect in such a new experience.

Jake's car smelled like leather. Not like an air freshener or old shoes or musty upholstery. But leather, cozy and inviting.

She'd rehearsed a few conversation starters over the course of the week, but none came to mind now. So when he started the car, she went to the only natural question she could think of. "Where are we going?"

He grinned. "It's a surprise."

A list of all the restaurants in Birch Harbor shuffled like a rolodex through her mind. Harbor Deli would be a disappointing choice. The pizzeria, too (even though she really loved pizza). The Bottle was a logical option, but that wouldn't quite make for a surprise. There was another handful of eateries sprinkled through town, any one of which might, in fact, catch her off guard. Especially if he picked a dive bar.

But then when they turned south onto Harbor Ave and wove down toward Birch Village, she wondered if Jake Hennings even knew what the word surprise meant.

"Okay," he said at last, parking in the small lot at the corner of where the road swept in a curve toward the Heirloom Inn. Clara peeked through the windshield, wondering if Sarah was there, getting ready for her beach party with Kate. If they only knew Clara was just yards away, on her own little adventure.

"Okay," Clara echoed.

Jake killed the ignition and said, "Wait right there."

She did as she was told, sitting as he disappeared behind

the car only to return to her door moments later. A piece of fabric in his hand.

"Now," he went on, his voice softening. Weakening. Wobbling. "I have to admit something." He held the fabric across his palms, limply. Awkwardly.

Clara frowned at it. Her stomach clenched, and a bullet of panic burst through her chest. She started shaking her head, but then he licked his lips and glanced nervously out at the water.

"Listen, Clara, this wasn't my idea."

CHAPTER 11—KATE

In the span of less than an hour, Kate had collected Sarah, stopped at The Bungalows so Sarah could get a change of clothes, returned to the Inn, grabbed the boat keys, and convinced her niece to ride out to the Island with her.

Initially, Sarah protested. She needed more time to get ready, she'd argued. She didn't know Vivi very well, she fibbed.

"Maybe now would be a good chance to bond?" Kate had offered.

That wasn't what convinced Sarah, however. What convinced her was learning that Matt was on his way to the Inn, and then Sarah would be stuck there, alone with him.

"Awkward," Sarah had complained, rushing into her new outfit and smearing on a second coat of eyeliner before joining Kate in the boat that bobbed in place at their private dock.

Kate had never once taken Matt's boat out without him. And though she had her own, a relic from Nora that had all but disintegrated in the boathouse, she preferred to be a passenger. Any time Matt invited her out, she sat along the back bench, the wind whipping her hair as she focused on her breathing.

"Put this on," Kate ordered Sarah as they launched, tossing a life jacket to her.

Sarah sulked. "Do I have to?"

"Of course you do. I've been privy to too many almost-drownings," Kate answered, adding, "Don't worry. I'll make Vivi wear one, too."

Sarah strapped herself in and took to the bench, stretching out her long, bare legs. It occurred to Kate that Sarah had no business being a misfit in Birch Harbor. She was beautiful and interesting, smart and confident.

So was Megan exaggerating?

Or had this dark-haired new girl really been eating her lunches in the bathroom? And if so, then why?

Kate opened her mouth to pry but thought better of it. Having raised two boys, she had learned that the best route to drag something out of a teenager was to listen, rather than talk. And she could only listen if Sarah had something to say. And Sarah wouldn't have anything to say, if she didn't have anything to talk about.

So, instead of commenting on the cooling temperatures or asking Sarah how she liked Birch Harbor and her teachers and the other students, she decided to change course.

Just as she pressed the throttle forward, she turned in her seat.

"You know what?" she asked Sarah.

"What?"

Kate let the boat idle, the loud sound dying off immediately. "Why don't you come sit here. I'm going to let you drive."

"I don't even drive a *car*," Sarah protested.

"You don't have your license?" Kate asked. She knew the answer. She remembered the day Megan called with celebratory news that Sarah passed the driver's test. Kate had even sent her a pair of fuzzy dice for the dashboard of her future car. When the Stevensons' world came crashing down, a new car for Sarah quickly fell by the wayside. Still, the girl did have her license. Any good aunt would know as much.

"Yes, I do have my license," Sarah answered, her curiosity piqued as she stood up from the bench and pawed her way along to Kate, unused to balancing in a boat.

"Then you can drive this, too," Kate waved Sarah into the seat.

"What if we get in trouble?"

"With whom?" Kate replied.

"My dad said that if you're under twenty-one, you need to take a class first."

"Oh, right," Kate answered, lifting her brow. She swallowed and considered this fact. When Kate was a kid, she and her sisters could drive their dad's boat as early as twelve years old. But had that even been legal? Now, she wasn't too sure.

She waffled. Was breaking the law worth gaining favor with her niece? Kate thought about Amelia, and what she would do. Maybe there was something to be said for letting loose every now and then.

"Well, I won't tell if you won't tell."

A small grin pricked at the corners of Sarah's mouth but quickly fell away. "What about Vivi?"

"Who's she going to tattle to?"

"Jake Hennings, maybe," Sarah answered.

Kate's eyes narrowed on her. "How do *you* know Jake Hennings?" she asked.

"He's Mercy's dad, remember?"

"Oh. Right."

"And Mercy is Vivi's best friend."

"Well, I'll talk to Vivi. She'll listen to me."

Sarah seemed to consider this. "Aunt Kate, you don't really know Vivi, do you?"

Kate frowned. "What are you talking about? *You're* the one who just said that *you* don't really know Vivi. If that's true, then how can *you* know that I *don't*?"

Sarah shook her head. "Never mind. Forget about it."

"Okay," Kate replied, keeping her inner thoughts to herself. Namely, that Sarah was talking in circles. Making excuses. Refusing to broaden her horizons and take a chance here or there.

If there was anything that Kate didn't want for Sarah, it was the life that Clara had been boxed into—a safe, dutiful life with few, if any friends and piles of extra credit towering on the corner of her nightstand after spending the afternoon scrubbing rental toilets at The Bungalows.

And while Kate ended up losing control over how Clara was raised, she still had an opportunity to take part in Sarah's upbringing. Even if just for a year.

"I'll handle Vivi. You drive," she directed, pointing to the throttle. "Now here is what you do."

Soon enough, they'd sputtered their way to Birch Bay, the Birch Harbor-facing side of Heirloom Island.

Kate tapped out a text to Matt's daughter that her ride

had arrived, and soon enough, they spotted Vivi—striding down her private dock, toward where Kate and Sarah sat in Matt's Bayliner.

"Did my dad say you could drive his boat?" Vivi asked with false sweetness as she climbed aboard, staring daggers at Sarah.

Kate blanched. It didn't occur to her that the vessel might be an element of jealousy. She glanced at Sarah, who was frozen by the younger girl's accusation.

"Yes," Kate answered quickly, punting. Committing to her bad decision and regretting it every step of the way but still struggling not to further alienate the two girls from one another. "And now it's your turn, Viv."

"E."

"What's that?" Kate asked.

"It's Viv-*i*. And I'm not allowed to drive. Not until I have my driver's license," she added.

Kate and Sarah exchanged a look. Either Vivi didn't know the law or Brian hadn't told Sarah the truth. Something in Kate's gut told her to trust Vivi on this one, and she suddenly felt more at ease about it all.

Knowing she had to act fast or else she'd ruin Sarah's night, Kate took a chance. One that she wasn't typically inclined to take. Not with a fifteen-year-old. Not with her boyfriend's daughter.

"Vivi, I'll let you drive the boat a little, if you'd like. I'll cover you, even. With your dad."

Vivi narrowed her gaze on Kate. "What if we get pulled over by the Marine Patrol?"

"Who, Jake?" Kate answered, half-joking.

"Jake Hennings? He's not Marine Patrol," Vivi replied evenly. "But he will be on the water tonight, that much is true." Something flickered in the girl's crystalline eyes. Something that caused Kate to hesitate. Instead of taking the bait, however, she ignored the comment.

"Tell you what, if Jake Hennings or anyone else pulls us over, I'll teach you girls how to flirt your way out of a ticket. Deal?"

That time, Vivi and Sarah exchanged a look.

Kate shook her head, good sense returning to her. "You know what, Vivi? You're right. You're too young. Neither one of you drives back. My mistake. I'll just take over. Here, Sarah. Get up."

She wasn't using reverse psychology on Vivi; really, she wasn't. Kate was sincere. Before everything else, Kate was a rule follower. Getting caught up in settling the differences among teenagers wasn't her forte, and though she may have been well-meaning, it was a dumb thing to do. It could compromise not only their safety, but also her own reputation.

But it was too late. Her strategy, inadvertently, had worked.

"No," Vivi answered. "If Sarah got to drive, then I get to drive. After all, if he let Sarah, then he'd let me, too."

"Here, I'll show you," Sarah scooted to the far inside of the seat, and Vivi squeezed in next to her.

Kate's breathing returned to normal, and she settled on the back bench, satisfied in somehow accomplishing the very goal she'd made for the short rendezvous to the Island.

The girls chatted easily. Kate tried to tune them out and give them a little space to find their way to friendship again. The age difference seemed irrelevant to Kate.

By the time they eased into the Hannigan dock, and Kate jumped out to tie the boat off, the girls were talking easily, their footing regained. Kate wondered if Sarah saw that it wasn't so bad to be friends with younger girls. It was better than nothing, especially if she was so dead set against spending time with Chloe or Paige.

"What time are you two meeting your friends?" Kate asked once they made it inside. She thought they might have broken off at the sea wall, meandering toward the Village to meet the others; instead, they'd followed her.

"Not for another ten minutes," Vivi answered. "Mercy is walking up from the South Cove now, though, so maybe she'll be early."

"You mean her dad isn't driving her here?" Sarah asked.

To Kate, it was an innocent question.

But to Vivi, clearly, it was an opening of some kind. She lifted her eyebrow at Sarah then glanced at Kate. "You Hannigans and your boy toys," she answered.

Taken aback, Kate dropped the boat keys on the counter and propped her hands on her hips, cocking her head. "*Excuse* me?"

Sarah folded her arms over her chest and stopped at the edge of the kitchen island, her eyes flying to Kate for help.

"What did you just say, Viviana?" She hated herself, a little bit, for using the girl's full name, as if she were her mother or something.

And she paid for it. Vivi's gaze settled like a fog on Kate, and she answered, "I said, 'you Hannigans and your boy toys.'" She pronounced each syllable like she was cracking an ice cube tray and plucking each block out, carefully so as not to burn herself from the freeze.

"And what is that supposed to mean?" Kate answered, her neck growing hot and her spine prickling.

As if snapped out of her trance, Vivi blinked then shook

her head before smiling sweetly. "Oh, I just mean it seems like each of you sort of... I don't know... sets her sights on a cute guy."

Kate nodded slowly, her gaze narrowed and hard. "And what does that have to do with Sarah's question?"

CHAPTER 12—AMELIA

As soon as Clara left for her date, Amelia called Michael, "I'm at my sister's cottage, and we found a locked drawer."

"Where? What do you mean you found a locked drawer?"

Even as she explained it, images of Nancy Drew flew through Amelia's mind. Soon enough, they'd solve the mystery and enjoy a burger and a milkshake on the beach together, ready to take on the next challenge. Then again, did Nancy have a handsome sidekick? Maybe. "Well, Clara dragged this little old vanity up from the basement. The front center drawer was locked."

She could hear his breath hitch, and it excited her. That Michael was as entrenched and interested in her family history as Amelia made her investigation of Wendell's fate not only manageable... but even enjoyable. She and Michael really were like a romantic pair of crimefighters, except there was no crime.

Not that they knew of, at least.

Her sisters had made fun of him, surmising that he must

be pretty bored to spend his extra time sorting through decades-old drama.

Megan, however, had come to Amelia and Michael's defense. "He's not bored," she'd said once over lunch when they were gossiping together. "He's *in love*."

And, he was, in fact. He'd admitted as much to Amelia. She loved him back, which at first was an odd thing for her. To settle in like that.

Sure, Amelia had told any number of men that she'd loved them: In the heat of a passionate kiss or during a walk in the park when another happy couple strolled past. The sentiment back then always felt like some desperate endgame, though.

Now, it felt like part of the process.

With Michael, love came in a natural, grown-up course of events. They had history together, for starters. Their shared status as Birch Harbor originals. Their high school days—awkward and delicate. Treacherous, perhaps. Sometimes living in Amelia's brain was like a threat to the present. Not that they had anything back then. Nothing romantic, for sure. Just the imbalanced relationship of a younger pretty girl and an older studious boy who saw each other in class and at parties. One party, at least.

Then came the past summer. First, their date at the lighthouse, the kiss, then a sequence of other dates—all around town and even out of town on daytrips. The dates turned quickly into his willingness to help her at the lighthouse. He had an affinity for local history, he'd revealed. No surprise there. His in-home library proved as much. But Amelia already knew about all that.

One day, when they were lounging around half-watching *Gone with the Wind* and half-cuddling, Amelia asked him, *"Why?"*

He'd replied, *"Why what?"*

"Why are you with me? Why are you helping me? Why do you love me?" The questions came out in a string just like that, and he laughed. Not a derisive laugh, but an affectionate one. One that told her she already knew why.

They were meant to be together. They were meant to bounce their insecurities off each other and find adventures and do all the things that soulmates did.

Later, when they were at his house and she stumbled separately into his library as he cooked dinner, she ran her hands along the books. Legal titles. Classics. Shakespeare, of course. And then, a section dedicated to all things Michigan and the Great Lakes. Nestled among them was a vertically shelved stack of pages, like printer paper stuffed between books to smooth the wrinkles. She'd been about to tug it out when he appeared in the doorway, summoning her for dinner.

He didn't see her, or if he did, he didn't reprimand her or ask her what she was looking at, but that slotted stack of white paper hung with her through all the dates and the I-Love-Yous and her sisters' niggling and Megan's defensiveness. She didn't ask about it, of course. She had no right. Not after what happened in that library so many years ago. If she asked about those white pages, then maybe that ill-fated night would come up, too. And what good would that do anyone?

Now, he replied to her answer. "Is Clara there with you? Did she try to open the drawer? Do you want my help?"

"No, no. Clara just left for her date, but we got it open before she did. Now here I am, and I just need to pull the darn thing open," she responded. "But I figured I'd let you know in case I find something, and it—" a thought occurred to her. "Oh, you know what, Michael? Just forget I even called. You have the Island school's case to worry about right now. You don't need more Hannigan drama."

"It's not *drama*, Amelia. It's interesting. But I do need to get to work. Say, if you do need something, call me back, all right?"

"All right, Michael," she answered. "Oh, and don't forget," she added. "Tomorrow at ten, we have our writing session." Amelia was referring to their plans to throw together a script for the re-enactment. Michael had agreed to consult and advise, as a sort of dramaturge, and her stage manager Lucy, had texted and confirmed she'd swing by to help, too.

"I'll be there with bells on," he assured her, and they ended their call.

Amelia set the phone down and eased into Clara's vanity chair, a wobbling, iron-framed thing with a tuffet and three uneven legs. Swallowing, she tucked her fingertips beneath the bottom lip of the drawer and slowly pulled it out.

Sitting inside was a Smith and Wesson snub-nose revolver.

The one Nora left to Amelia.

The one that was her father's.

The one that never belonged to him in the first place.

CHAPTER 13—CLARA

Night was beginning to fall on the marina as Jake explained why, exactly, he needed to *blindfold* Clara.

"It was *Mercy's* idea," he went on.

Clara's frown deepened, and her eyes dropped again to the piece of fabric—a red bandana, she now could see. "Mercy said you should *blindfold* me?" she managed meekly, bewildered. Maybe dating apps and coffee meetups were the way to go after all. Then again, there was something sweet about a man who took dating tips from his teenage daughter.

"Well, yes," he answered, grinning sheepishly. "That was part of her idea. Now you need to step out of the car," he instructed, holding the door wide for her.

Something in his tone suggested her instincts were wrong. That her gut reaction was all wrong. That she had no reason to be nervous and every reason to be excited.

She got out of the car, rising and smoothing her dress, her eyes darting past him to the Inn, half-praying that Kate would tear out of there and sprint over... and half-praying that Kate wasn't even home to see what was taking shape at the parking lot near the marina.

On the path that trickled from the Inn to Birch Village, Clara spotted a throng of teenagers. Sarah and her friends, no doubt. Maybe Mercy was there, too. And Vivi. Maybe there would be a witness to this little thrill.

"What else did Mercy suggest?" Clara asked.

Jake replied, "It's a surprise, like I said."

Clara laughed, but his grin slipped, and he looked like sweat might pour off his forehead. Shaking his head, he dropped the bandana and rubbed his fingers into his eyes. "This is incredibly awkward. I'm sorry."

"No, no," Clara assured. "This is *great*. I'm not used to surprises, that's all." Her voice wobbled as she said it. It was true. The last big surprise in her life had come down from the annals of her deceased mother. It would be a good thing to have a more pleasant surprise now. A sweet one.

He nodded helplessly, and Clara's heart throbbed with affection.

She turned around and faced the opposite direction.

"What are you doing?" Jake asked.

"I'm ready to be surprised," she replied.

She could sense Jake's arms rise and fall around her, encircling her as he pulled the fabric over her eyes loosely. Silently grateful she'd opted for waterproof makeup, she smiled as she felt him tie the bandana at the back of her head.

"Is that okay?" he asked. His voice came close to her ear, and she inadvertently leaned into it, nodding.

"Okay, I'll just lead the way now."

One hand traced down her arm, collecting her fingers in his palm and pressing his other hand into her lower back.

She let him guide her, and though she knew the area

well, discombobulation set in immediately. He turned her left and right. Down a path, up a short set of stairs and down another. Up and down again, like a game. Wood transitioned to stone beneath her feet. Then grass. Then wood.

It felt as if they were near the water. She could smell the lake, feel the cool wet air. In all likelihood, he was leading her north along the Village toward The Bottle, which sat at the very far end, closer to the lighthouse than to the Inn, almost—farther from one sister and closer to the next. She wasn't used to having her sisters surround her like that.

Now that they were back, would Clara ever escape the hovering threat of her family?

Did she even want to?

"Okay, Clara," Jake murmured. "The only way for me to do this and keep some semblance of surprise is to lift you up. Is that all right?"

"Lift me up?" Panic gripped her briefly. "Like, how? What do you mean?"

"Like this," he whispered again, scooping beneath her as her legs swung up and her head fell back, and in spite of herself, she laughed. A heartfelt, giddy laugh.

"Wow," she managed. "Count me surprised, because I can't think of a place in all of Birch Harbor where you'd need to sweep me up into the air."

Squeezing her eyes shut so she couldn't catch a glimpse through the loose bottom edge of the bandana, Clara took a deep breath.

"Then you haven't been on the right dates," he answered, his voice low.

Gone was the smell of the lake. In its place, leather, perhaps. And cologne. Clean soap and a warm musk, but it wasn't her surroundings Clara was breathing in.

It was him.

JAKE SAT her in a plastic chair at what felt like a folding table. Not the hardy wooden bar-height stools of The Bottle. Or a high-backed booth in some dive off Harbor Ave.

The floor seemed to rock beneath her feet. If Clara didn't know better, she'd have thought they were adrift in the middle of the lake. Either that, or her blindfold and the presence of this handsome man had disabled her balance entirely, leaving Clara floating blindly.

"Are you ready?" he asked.

She nodded, her eyes still closed and covered.

He worked slowly to unknot the back, then braced a hand on her shoulder as the fabric slid away, and Clara opened her eyes.

At first, she didn't know where she was or what she was seeing. Then she squinted, and the landscape and setting came into focus. "We *are* in the water?" she whispered more to herself than to him as her gaze swept across Lake Huron and settled on a set table in front of her.

"Welcome aboard the Birch Bell," he answered, lifting his hand about them.

She gripped the table, rocking involuntarily forward, then braced herself and stood. "We're on the *ferry*?" Clara gasped.

He grinned and nodded. "We have it for exactly two hours."

Clara clutched at her chest. "I never would have guessed," she said through a breathy voice. And it occurred to her that she was in a big heap of trouble. "Jake, do you realize what you've done?"

Frowning, he rounded the table and stood behind his seat. Between them, a plate of crackers and cheese and one with sliced fruit and vegetables sat waiting. Chips and salsa took up one corner, and a bowl of salad with plastic wrap pinched around stainless tongs took up another. In a small cooler next to the table, its lid propped open, were water bottles and cans of Arizona Iced Tea. It was a hodge-podge of a meal—maybe Mercy had planned it out, too (no real main course, just snacks), but Clara realized if it were any fancier, she might need to expect a proposal.

"What have I done?" Jake asked.

"You've set the bar," Clara replied. "I pity the fool who has to follow this." She spread her hand across their table and out to the sunset-kissed water.

"Well, maybe there won't be one," he replied, grinning mischievously.

"Won't be one what?" she asked.

"A fool who has to follow?" he winced, but she glowed inside, laughing with him at the lame joke but inwardly taken.

Sitting back down, she propped her chin in one hand and let her eyes follow him. "Maybe you're right."

It was unusual for Clara to date at all, much less go out with a slightly older man with a daughter. And one as good looking as Jake. Even so, she felt immediately comfortable in his presence. Protected. Safe. Despite the fact they were teetering on the upper deck of the Birch Bell.

He sat too, shaking his head. "It's nothing, really. I mean, I basically brought you to my job."

His backtracking was adorable, and Clara realized that was as good an ice-breaker conversation as any. She answered, "Tell me about it."

"My job?"

"Yes," she replied. "Like, what is the craziest thing you've seen out here?"

CHAPTER 14—KATE

When Matt arrived back at the Inn, the girls had just left for the beach, arm in arm, their relationship rejuvenated. Kate wasn't certain this was a good thing, after all.

"I had an odd interaction with Vivi," she said to him as she poured two glasses of wine.

"What happened?" he asked, accepting his glass and following her to the back porch. It had become their routine. A drink with a view of the lake each night. Sometimes, her guests would be out there, too. If that were the case, she and Matt would move down to the shoreline and walk together, offering themselves and the visitors more privacy.

She answered lightly. "Oh, I don't know. I might have been imagining it." Maybe she was. After all, Sarah didn't much seem to mind Vivi's implication that she had a crush on Jake. Then again, Jake Hennings was quite a looker. Maybe any girl in Birch Harbor would admit to having a harmless crush on him.

Maybe he was *that* dad. The hot one. Lately, tunnel vision on Matt had set in. He was the only hot dad in her life. Maybe she'd better open her eyes a little. If not for her own benefit, for Clara and Sarah's.

But it wasn't only Vivi's implication that Sarah had a crush on Jake that rubbed Kate wrong. It was also Vivi's implication that Kate and her sisters were only around to swoop in on local men. As if they were black widows.

"What was it?" Matt pressed, lowering his glass once they were seated, alone, on the outdoor loveseat.

Kate set her gaze on the water, debating whether she ought to stick her nose into Matt's parenting. Would she have wanted that? If one of the boys was exhibiting such behavior, would Kate want a close friend to speak up? She liked to think so. She raised her hands. "Okay, well, this is just *my* observation. I might be way off base."

"I can handle it," Matt answered.

Kate eyed him, then pushed on. "Okay, first thing's first. Vivi is so smart, Matt. *Very* smart. And she's beautiful. And I know she has a good heart."

"Cut to the chase, Kate. What happened?"

Blinking, Kate answered point blank, "She has a problem with you and me being together." Matt took a deep breath and crossed his arms. She added quickly, "But I expected that, of course." Matt started to reply, but Kate held up her hand and lowered her chin, focusing on him with as serious and calm an expression as she could muster. "It's not just with me, though. She said something along the lines of, *all you Hannigan women do is chase men.*"

Matt's face fell into a deep frown, and Kate pressed her mouth into a thin line. Maybe she shouldn't have said anything. What good would it do?

"That's offensive," Matt replied simply. "I'll talk to her."

"No, no. I don't want you to talk to her, I just... I just wanted to air it out, I guess."

"No, I'm going to talk to her, Kate. She has no right to be rude."

Kate felt herself backtracking involuntarily, rationalizing what she'd just reported. "She's uncomfortable. Her dad is dating again, and that's awkward for any girl. Especially a teenager. Talking to her will make it worse," Kate reasoned.

"But she can't get away with treating people like that," Matt replied. "Especially *you*."

"Well, can we let this one slide? I really only mentioned it to vent. You know? Anyway, teenage girls can be like that, Matt. Trust me, I know."

He seemed to consider this point, taking a long sip of his drink and remaining quiet for a few moments. Kate thought back to when Ben and Will were in high school. How different it was to see the experience of a teenage boy compared to her own experience with sisters and girl-friends. And now the interactions of the next generation of Birch Harbor teen queens.

"I know, too," he muttered, letting out a long sigh. "I know, too."

Kate debated whether to press him, but it was a hard decision. Maybe he had something he wanted to air out, too?

"Do you want to talk about it?" she asked, her voice soft. Open.

Matt flicked a glance to Kate, then pulled a face. "Well, okay."

Kate shifted her weight away from him and opened her shoulders, setting her glass down on the table and resting her hands in her lap. "I'm all ears." Maybe they'd stay ahead of the drama. Maybe she was right to mention Vivi's comment and open the door to discussing how things might go as Matt and Kate's relationship grew more and more serious.

He uncrossed his arms and ran his hands down the thighs of his shorts, meeting her gaze at last. "Vivi had some friend trouble when she lived with her mom. Nothing too serious, at first. Teasing, mostly. She seemed to find a fault with everyone and point it out. Even when she was little. Her mom didn't want to deal with it. When Vivi was in sixth grade, she revealed one of her best friend's secrets to a whole group of boys. I don't even know the secret. It was something stupid that happened at a sleepover. Like the poor girl burped or laughed so hard, soda blew out of her nose."

Kate winced. For the girl and for Matt. Even for Vivi.

"Anyway, the girl's mom made a big fuss about *bullying*, and Vivi's mom just, well, gave up." Matt lifted his hands and dropped them in his lap. "So, the next year, I decided Vivi would live with me. Vivi took this to mean that her mom was kicking her out, but that's not true. She just didn't know what to do about it. Didn't have time. Work, social life —those things got in the way of my ex's ability to raise Vivi the right way, I guess. Now it's been over two years since she came to Heirloom, but I'm still trying to undo the past fourteen."

"It's not your fault her mom let her become a mean girl," Kate interjected.

"Of course, it's my fault." A shadow crossed his face, and Kate almost felt him glare at her. "It's my fault that I didn't make it work with Vivi's mom. It's my fault I didn't see her tendencies earlier and clamp down. You know, before the divorce, I mean."

Kate shook her head. "Matt, you're doing the best you can now. That's what matters. She has four years left here. At *least*. You can do a lot with those four years."

"What were you girls like?"

"Hmm?" she asked, lifting her glass to her lips.

"You and your sisters? I never remember you or Amelia being cruel to other girls. Did Megan turn out that way? What about Clara?"

In his question, she read a subtle accusation. As though some insidious quality was a trait passed down through the Hannigan family lines. After all, Nora was known for having a cutting way about her. An insincerity despite her magnetic personality. Or because of it.

"What are you saying?" Kate asked, frowning.

"Nothing." Matt shook his head. "I'm sorry. Nothing about you or your family. Not at all. I just want to better understand women, I guess. And my role with Viv. You know?"

Kate considered this. "Well, you knew me. That wasn't my style. I was always too afraid of getting in trouble to be mean to anyone." She laughed lightly. "And I think Clara was the same."

At that, Matt grinned. "She took after both of us, I guess. I hope?"

Kate smiled back and took his hand. "Somehow, I think so."

"Are we always going to be stuck in limbo with Clara? Will she *ever* want to... get to know me?"

"Oh, I think she'll come around, yes. In fact, Clara *needs* to get to know you. It's the one thing that will help her move away from her past, if that even makes sense."

"Was it hard on her?"

"Growing up with Nora for a mother?"

He shook his head. "Growing up without a dad."

"I think both were hard. But Clara is who she is despite that. She likes her quiet life. She likes her job. Her little house, of course. I think she's in a better place now. I think she'll come to you in time. I really do. Especially now that —" Kate's words fell away as the lights from the Birch Bell caught her eye out in the distance on the lake. "Wow," she breathed. "I've never seen it lit up like that."

Matt followed her gaze. "Oh, that's right." His eyes brightening.

"What?" she asked. "Matt." Kate gave him a look. "Fess up."

"I wasn't supposed to tell," he replied, the corner of his mouth lifting. "But Vivi told me that Jake Hennings planned to take his date out on the ferry tonight."

"Clara is his date," Kate answered, confused.

"I know." Matt laughed, then added, "Vivi doesn't know I know that part. She just told me that he asked Mercy and Vivi to help him plan it. She wouldn't tell me who he was taking, but I already knew, of course. Good for them. Good for *him*."

Kate returned her gaze to the boat, a rush of warmth flooding her heart. "Vivi helped him plan it?"

If that was true, then maybe Kate's suspicions were all wrong. Maybe she was being sensitive. Maybe Vivi wasn't a mean girl, just a sad one. A jealous one, even. And maybe Clara was having the time of her life out there on the water with the handsome Jake Hennings.

"Yep, that's what she said."

"Well, if she shared that with you, Matt, then I'd say you're on top of the whole 'raising a teen girl' thing."

He grinned and settled back into the loveseat. "You think so?"

"I know so," Kate answered, taking his hand again, as they resumed their normal. A relaxing conversation, free of all the drama that Kate so desperately hoped wouldn't consume her as summer turned to fall and things shifted again in Birch Harbor.

"So, you never told me. What was Megan like when she was in high school?"

Kate sighed. "Megan was a bit of a rebel, I think. But only at home. She wore black when Mom wanted her to wear white. She cut her hair when Mom wanted it long. But at school, she kept her head down and followed directions. She dated a lot. I know that. She loved to go on dates. They never amounted to anything, which cracked me up. It's like she enjoyed the thrill of it but not the hard work. Of course, that was high school. Once she met Brian, well... I think they've figured it out. You know?"

Matt nodded. "He's a good guy. Smart. They're going to be successful."

"I agree," Kate said. They would, too. Especially since they were going to build a second space to house winter events. Things would go well for Megan and Brian. It would take time. And it would be hard, but they'd pull it off. Kate knew they would.

"And Amelia? I'll always have this picture of her as a kid among adults, sort of elbowing her way into the heart of things. She liked to be seen."

"Yes, she did. Still does, I think."

"That was your mom. I see it in Vivi, too. A need for... attention, I guess?"

"From men, especially." Even as Kate said it, she felt like she was betraying Amelia. She added quickly, "Amelia always put family first, though. I remember back then—when I got... pregnant—" Saying the word now somehow felt crude, and Kate tried in vain to shake it, pushing ahead. "She was bound and determined to save me. Fiercely protective. Almost like she would risk everything just for me."

CHAPTER 15—AMELIA

1992

It was May. The school musical was weeks away, and Amelia already knew all of her lines. The drama teacher, Mrs. Finch, was still scavenging for props.

Kate had recently dropped the bomb about her pregnancy, and plans were in motion to whisk her away to another state so that Amelia and Megan could go on living their lives and enjoying their summer on the lake.

Still, even as a solution developed between their parents and Kate, tensions were high at the Hannigan household, and Amelia spent every last moment at school, hanging around in the theater with her friends, making them laugh, practicing scenes, finding a good hallway alcove in which to sing at the top of her lungs to catch that perfect reverberation she'd need to pull off Sister Sarah Brown.

Yes.

Freshman phenom Amelia Hannigan was starring as Sarah Brown in *Guys and Dolls*.

It was the role of a lifetime, she was certain. And Mrs.

Finch was desperate to make it perfect. After all, the woman was retiring that June after a forty-year career teaching young thespians.

They had most of the set underway. Now it was time to pull together the last of the minor props and start dress rehearsals.

But there were other things going on at school, too. Ever since the party at the house on the harbor, no one knew where they were going to get together every weekend.

And that was the essence of teenage life in Birch Harbor —weekend parties.

In the summer, it was easy enough—everyone just met on the beach.

During the school year, they stuck to indoor gatherings as much as possible since the temps dropped so much. Now, summer was upon them again, but no one dared host a party on the beach before Memorial Day Weekend. It was tradition, after all.

Amelia begged her parents to reconsider their blanket ban on having any friends over to the house, but that fight was futile. And anyway, she was just a ninth grader. She had no ability to plan a large-scale high school party.

With the star quarterback, Matt Fiorillo, also grounded, it left a whole school full of kids without anywhere to go. Without anywhere to dance and play music and find a love connection for the weekend—or the semester.

Normally, such a monumental responsibility wouldn't fall on the shoulders of a ninth-grade drama geek. But with rumors circulating about her older sister (unbeknownst to frantic Nora), Amelia knew she needed to clear the air and set the record straight. She had a chance to prove that the Hannigan sisters were still cool. Still normal. Definitely not pregnant. And she was going to see to it that she and Kate would sneak out and show up at a party the very next weekend—flat stomachs and happy smiles. She would do it for her sister. Before things went too far.

So, that's when Amelia turned to the upper-classman boy who sat behind her in the history elective. He was a jock-scholar who hung around the periphery of the popular crowd. Somewhat disinterested and indifferent enough to maintain a stable social status, despite his leanings toward geekery.

Amelia, whose interest was split between drama and an eighteen-year-old guitarist who played gigs at the Village every Thursday night, had a feeling that the brooding history class boy might have liked her. At least, he was always offering to help her with homework or study together for quizzes. And Amelia identified as something of a nerd anyway—a drama nerd, which was a little different than a history nerd, but still.

One day, out of the blue, in the middle of a video about the moon landing, she tore a corner from her notebook page and scrawled out a note.

What are you doing this weekend?

She balled it up, pretended to yawn, twisted left, and popped the little wad of paper onto his desk.

And the very next weekend, there she was. At a big, fancy house in Harbor Hills.

She couldn't remember seeing much of the boy that night. Mainly, she stuck with her drama friends. But at one point, one of them unearthed this gangster-movie-style gun. In the library, where they weren't supposed to be, in some nook or cranny—Amelia didn't know *where* he found it. She hadn't been watching. The weapon obviously belonged to the boy's dad, and it even seemed more like a relic than a weapon. But still.

"We can use it for that scene in the play!" one of them cheered, swinging it around dangerously.

Amelia grew nervous. "Dude, put it back. We could get in trouble."

"No way. It's *perfect* for *Guys and Dolls*. Don't you think?" He swung it again, rattling off his lines just as the door to the library opened.

Scared to death they would be found out, Amelia grabbed the gun and tucked it into the back of her jeans on a whim.

Sure enough, there he stood at the door.

The boy.

Michael Matuszewski.

There was no chance to return the gun anywhere in the library, and the boy watched Amelia and her friends like a hawk for the rest of the party. She wound up leaving early, backing through the door like a cartoon character or something. If she'd been a little smarter, she'd have dropped it in a flowerpot on her way out. Or she'd have shipped it. But even then, Michael would know. He sensed something about her. Amelia knew it.

What happened next sent Amelia into a week-long illness, vacillating between headaches and nausea like *she* was the pregnant one in the family.

If her father or mother had ever found her with a gun in the house, they'd send Amelia off to Arizona, too.

So, stupidly, she kept it in her backpack, hidden.

Then, days later at school, a new rumor took shape.

In some ways, it was a welcome reprieve for the older two Hannigan sisters.

Amelia owns a gun!

She brings it to school!

Somehow, the minor detail that one of the other drama

kids had first grabbed it out of the Matuszewski library faded into the ether. The new truth was that Amelia had become a psychopath, naturally.

The good thing was that any talk of Kate having lost her virginity was old news. The hivemind had buzzed past that now.

The bad thing was that, well, Amelia was branded a psychopath with a gun, of course. This complicated matters, because there was no way in *hell* she'd give it up to her parents. If she did that, she and Kate would both be big, fat disappointments in addition to scourges of Birch Harbor High.

And there was no way she could simply return the gun to the Matuszewski home. Despite his cooperation with the party, she still hardly knew Michael. What if his lawyer dad had her arrested? Anyway, Harbor Hills was a gated community. Plus, she sat *in front* of Michael in class, not conveniently behind him. Even so, Amelia remained hopeful that she could find a moment to secretly slip the stupid relic into the Matuszewski mailbox or even Michael's locker, somehow.

But she never got the chance.

Someone told on her.

And soon enough, she was sitting in the office of the Birch Harbor High School principal:

Mr. Gene Carmichael.

CHAPTER 16—MEGAN

Megan and Brian stopped for a slice of pizza before heading back home. Another full day of work lay ahead of them—detailing plans for their as-of-yet unnamed fall event taking priority. But Megan had also promised Amelia she'd take a look at the script they wrote for the re-enactment.

If she were being honest, Megan had low expectations of the lighthouse opening. She'd never say as much to her older sister. It'd crush Amelia's dreams, of course. Still, the whole thing seemed too quirky. Too oddball. Too Amelia, maybe.

But that was precisely the reason Megan agreed to help. And it was the reason she nagged Kate and Clara to help, too.

If all three of the more down-to-earth sisters took a look at Amelia's plans, maybe they could shape it up into something that might not be dismissed as the latest town spectacle, brought to you by the town looney.

During dinner, Brian settled Megan's question about Amelia and Michael. *What does Michael see in Amelia? What could a stable, quiet, serious, lawyer see in funky, off-beat, transient Amelia?*

"Whatever he sees in her, it's a good thing," he said. "Amelia is fun loving and warm."

"And pretty and interesting," Megan added, feeling silly for suggesting anything else earlier. "It's just that they're sort of opposites, though. You know?"

"Opposites can attract," Brian pointed out.

"Ooh," Megan replied. "That's not a bad name for a future event."

Inspired, Megan shifted the conversation squarely onto their business brainstorming, a new favorite focus for both of them. Megan pulled her notepad from her purse. "We really do need to nail something down for a title."

"Okay." Brian steepled his fingers and put on a serious expression. "Are we sticking with the letter *F*?"

"Yes," Megan replied. "And I still like *Flirting into Fall*," Megan said, referring to the name she'd coined on the drive down to the Village.

"Too young and too... I don't know. Girly? You're going to lose the men with that one," Brian answered, clearing away their drinks as the server poised a steaming pepperoni pizza on the iron stand in the center of the table. They both thanked him, then Brian went on, "You know, Megan, what's wrong with keeping it simple? Why not *Fall Festival*?"

"Too generic. Married people will show up thinking we're a farmer's market or something."

"Does it have to have alliteration?" Brian asked. "You're boxing yourself in if you have to have alliteration."

Megan raised a slice to her mouth and took a bite, considering his point. At last, she swallowed and nodded. "Yes. We started with it. It's our branding, now. And I think it sets us apart, you know?"

He shrugged and took his own bite, chewing with a thoughtful expression. "*Autumn Affections*?"

"Weird," Megan replied, still adding it to the list. That was their process. Judge aloud but jot it all down.

Brian turned his head to the window. "I wonder how Sarah's little party is going?"

"I can't believe she agreed to go," Megan answered. "She's been so... *moody* lately. Like a premature recluse."

"Do you think it's safe?"

"What? To have a moody teenager? No, actually. I don't. But what choice do we have?" She grinned at Brian, who laughed and shook his head.

"These lake parties. Or 'beach' parties," he drew air quotes.

"Hey, no mocking," Megan answered. "And yeah. I mean, didn't you go to parties in high school?"

Nodding his head, he swallowed another bite before answering. "Our parties weren't on the *water*. It scares me a little, you know? It's dark out there, and..." He paused then met Megan's stare. "Has a kid ever drowned?"

Megan frowned. "Not that I know of. I mean, it's not like they're drinking. And the marina is well-lit. Plus, they usually do a bonfire, you know."

"I don't really like it, Megan. I think it's too risky."

She didn't disagree, and now her stomach was churning. "Should we call her and tell her to go home?"

Brian turned his head back to Megan. "Send her a text to check in. But after tonight, let's put a soft halt on the water-front parties."

"Well, summer is over, so there won't be many more. Maybe there won't be any more, actually." Megan racked her brain. "When we were kids, we didn't hang out on the beach after Labor Day. It was tradition to move the parties to houses."

"And parents allowed that?" Brian raised an eyebrow.

"Not really. They were always secret parties."

"Almost as bad as lake parties, then," he answered.

"You mean 'beach?'" She curled her fingers into air quotes, mocking him and smiling. "Well, kids don't have a place to hang out in Birch Harbor, you know?"

Brian snapped his fingers. "That's it, Meg," he said, his eyes lighting up.

"What's it?" She dropped her crust onto her plate and wiped her fingers on a napkin.

"The field."

"What about it?"

He grabbed her hands across the table. "We'll let Sarah host parties on *the field.*"

The idea struck her brain like a bell, chiming to life a litany of possibilities. Nodding slowly, her mouth turned up in a slow grin. "I love it. *Perfect*, Brian. Between events, any weekend we don't have something planned, Megan can have the place for high school get-togethers or parties or whatever."

"Do we chaperone?" Brian asked, tentative.

Megan considered this. "Do we chaperone their lake parties?"

"Good point," he replied, bringing a finger to his lips and nibbling on his nail. "Well, it's a start. Let's pitch it to Sarah. The good thing is, no more secret house parties while parents are gone. And no drowning."

Megan nodded and took another slice of pizza.

"But the bad thing is," Brian went on, "parties in the woods can be just as bad as parties on the lake."

"Not if we know about it," Megan reasoned through bites. "Consider this: we know about the lake parties. All parents do. All *locals* do. They're effectively public, which adds that safety net. It's the secret house parties where things get out of control. Kids get into trouble because they have the privacy factor. The hidden factor. If we give Sarah the field, then she and her friends know that we *know* about the party. It's all you need. That accountability. Plus, no water."

"True," Brian agreed. "I suppose the next step is just to make sure kids will actually show up."

"And how do we do that?" Megan asked. "Sarah lost her shot to be a social leader when she split apart from her little summer group. Remember? Paige and Chloe? Mercy and Vivi? They all idol-worshipped her. Now, she's on the outside."

Brian stared back outside the window, his eyes focusing on something in the distance.

She followed his gaze to see a pack of kids moving up the shoreline, an offshoot of the high school group, no doubt. He answered at length, "I don't think so. Look."

Megan craned her neck to get a better vantage point from her side of the table. Then, narrowing her eyes on the group of kids, Megan recognized Sarah there. It was always a little thrill to see your child wandering in her own parallel universe—out in public or somewhere apart from her parents. And there she was now, laughing and walking with those same girls she'd effectively broken up with just a week prior.

"I guess that's how it goes when you're young," Megan murmured.

"What do you mean?" Brian asked.

"Friendship is fluid like that. Grudges don't last." Megan wasn't convinced Sarah ever held a grudge against Vivi or vice versa, but teenage drama was like seaweed—washing in and out, a rubbery net hiding beneath a moving blanket of water.

"Did they have a fight or something? What exactly happened, anyway?"

Megan sucked in a breath. Sarah had divulged her secret to Megan alone. A daughter confiding in her mother.

So far, it could stay that way. A secret.

But Megan knew she needed to keep her eye on the situation. It was one thing to protect your child's trust.

It was another to forsake your family's reputation.

Just as she was about to reply to Brian, her phone rang.

CHAPTER 17—CLARA

"The craziest thing I've seen?" Jake echoed her question wistfully, filling her glass three-quarters full. He'd revealed a chilled bottle of wine, nestled secretly in the ice chest, and it was too late for her to decline. Maybe one little drink wouldn't hurt, anyway. Now he went on, answering her question about the most exciting parts of his job. "I haven't been here *that* long. It's only my second full summer, you know."

"Right," she replied easily, tasting the sweet white Zin and considering the fact that maybe she *did* like wine after all. Was that the turning point from young adult to full-fledged grownup? You suddenly liked the taste of wine?

"Okay, I got it. This is an easy one, actually."

She grinned and took another sip. This one longer. "Go on," she replied.

"My first year out here, I got a lot of flak from locals. I felt a little like that geeky scientist in *Jaws*."

She shrugged. "Haven't seen it in years. Since I was a kid, probably."

"Oh," he answered. "Well, you should really watch it again. It's a *classic*, Clara."

Each time he used her name, her heart beat a little faster. "Well, maybe we can watch it together sometime?" She twisted her hands in her lap beneath the table.

"I'd love that. Maybe on our second date?"

"Second date?" she replied, dipping her chin. "We haven't even finished our first."

"Do we have to wait until it's over to decide?"

She shook her head.

He took another sip. "So, anyway. In the movie, Richard Dreyfuss is this smarty-pants biologist called out to help with the shark problem. But, of course, the hardened locals write him off." Jake frowned, then shook a finger at her, "Actually, I think I'm more like *Brody*. The police chief—"

"But you *were* a marine biologist," Clara reasoned then laughed and threw her hands up. "I don't even know the movie! I have no idea what I'm talking about."

"Well, I'm both of them. I'm the likable police chief who wants to protect the town even if he isn't an islander, and I'm the clever marine biologist who has enough gumption to tell the locals they can stick it where the sun doesn't shine."

"Ouch," Clara replied, pressing her hands to her chest and feigning injury to her heart.

"Sorry," Jake answered. "I guess you'd be the local in that scenario, huh?"

Clara nodded, and a coy grin cracked through her lips. "You do sound like quite a guy, though. Caring but strong."

He chuckled. "I'm just kidding. I love that movie. It was probably a factor in my career choice, you know. And then again in my career change. Studying and teaching marine biology is a lot different than living on the water." After another swig, he went on, "Anyway, when you asked about the craziest thing—well, that's what came to mind. That local versus outsider conflict. Or old guard versus new hand, I suppose. Because my first year here, we had a boating accident that threw me right into it." He pointed a finger toward the shoreline of Heirloom Cove. "Some tourists rented a couple of our stock. One took a jet ski, the other a rowboat. Then they proceeded to get drunk. Or maybe they were already drunk. I'm not sure. It was a big party, and they made their way around the lake then down south on the cove, I guess. *I* wasn't working when they took out the rentals." He gave her a knowing eye as if to suggest it was only ever the local deckhands stupid enough to rent out vessels to drunkards or frat boys—whoever the scoundrels may have been.

"Were they okay?" Clara asked, thumbing through her memory for news of the incident.

"Yeah, actually. They did have life jackets on. I think they walked away with nothing more than well-earned seasickness, truth be told."

Clara finished another sip of wine. This one even longer than the others. "That's probably why I didn't hear about it then. We don't get much news about what happens on the lake, unless it's some huge tragedy."

"Right, well, the *people* were okay, but the jet ski was beat up, and—here's the kicker—" he leaned, in, his arms crossed on the table "—the rowboat was so badly damaged that by the time the Marine Patrol got out there, it had sunk."

"Ooh," Clara replied. "A sunken ship." She liked where this was going. If he made it any spookier, she'd have to spring across the table and into his arms until he comforted her worried heart. She grinned to herself and wiggled to the edge of her seat.

"Well, that all happened before I got to the scene. It was a Sunday, and I was off work," Jake went on. "When I finally got there, after the jet ski was returned and the drunks were arrested, I arranged for the patrol to bring a standby vessel and a couple of divers."

"Why?" Clara's eyes grew wide. "Was one of the drunks still down in the *boat*?" Her voice raised in a high pitch, and Jake laughed, waving her off.

"No, no. I told you. They were *fine*. I'm talking about raising the boat back up and salvaging it."

"But wouldn't it be useless?" she pressed, fascinated now. Clara had heard about a sunken barge up north of town and other ships across Lake Huron that had met the same fate. As far as she knew, they just stayed down there, turning into part of the lakebed like accessories in a fishbowl.

"Not so we could save the *boat*," Jake answered, his eyes turning to fire. "So we could save the..." He leaned away and spread his hands out, glancing right and left and stumbling over his words, "So we could save the... *lake*. The earth!" He laughed at himself.

Clara tilted her head at him sympathetically and smiled. "Oh, I see. Right, of course. I guess I never thought about that."

"Sunken vessels are a big factor in marine pollution," he added, downing the rest of his drink and centering the empty glass between his hands, studying it. "Anyway," his eyes flitted back up to hers, "Marine Patrol called me crazy. *It's just a rowboat!* they said. And they were right. It's not like it was a steamboat or even this baby right here." He waved his hand around them again, indicating the ferry.

"I see your point. But would it be easy to do? To drag the boat back up?"

"Well, yes and no. There's a system for pulling them up,

you see. But they were right. You need *two* certified divers, and you need to dedicate time and a standby vessel and crew—which we could have used the Bell, but then there are the regulations the Marine Patrol has in place. It can get murky."

"No pun intended?" Clara joked.

Jake cracked a smile. "Anyway, they branded me a newbie and a dreamer, and I haven't quite regained the respect of the Marine Patrol."

"And the rowboat is still down there?" Clara asked.

"Oh yeah," Jake replied. "We never touched it again."

"Could you, though?"

"Could I what?"

"Dive to it? Like Ariel in *The Little Mermaid* or something?"

Jake laughed. "Haven't seen it in years," he answered wryly.

Clara blushed but narrowed her eyes on him. "You should watch it again. It's a *classic*, Jake."

He laughed hard, and now they were both leaning in across the table, their hands just inches apart.

"So could you?" she asked again.

"Dive down there? Well, yeah. I could. I'm certified. But it's pointless. It was a rental. There's nothing valuable, and it's just a piece of aluminum. It's done its damage, and I'd have no one to go with." He glanced away. "Anyway, Marine Patrol was right. It's not a big deal."

"Sounds like it could be fun, though."

"Diving down to a sunken rowboat?"

"Romantic, even?" Clara squinted, the sunset bouncing around him and into her eyes, but she squeezed them shut quickly and shook her head, cringing inwardly. "That was super cheesy."

"Tell you what," Jake flipped his hands over, palms up on the table. Involuntarily, almost, Clara slid hers onto his, and then there they were: sitting on top of the Birch Bell, holding hands.

"What?" she replied, meeting his gaze and tucking her lips between her teeth, ready for whatever he said next. Whatever he *did* next.

"Let's get you certified, and I'll take you there."

"You'll take me on a dive down to the bottom of Lake Huron?" As she said it aloud, she realized it sounded like something she would never do in her whole life. Something she had zero interest in. But now, she had every ounce of interest in doing just that. Risking her life on a fool's errand.

"Yes," he answered. "I'll take you wherever you want to go, in fact."

Clara's eyes lit up, but then her smile faded away. "It's getting late in the year. Is anyone around here still doing SCUBA lessons?" In Birch Harbor each summer, the marina hired at least one diving instructor who ran weekly clinics and private lessons. Clara didn't know much more than that since she'd spent so little time on the marina. Mainly, she'd just seen glimpses of the diving students or instructor sinking into the lake at an empty spot on the shore north of the Village or sometimes south down the cove.

"I am," Jake answered.

"*You* teach SCUBA?" Clara's eyes grew wide. "I've never seen you out there, though."

"I don't do it for the town. But I have my certifications. My license." His face lit up, and Clara pressed her lips together, rethinking everything she knew about the world— that it was bigger than she realized. About dating—that it could be *fun*. About herself—that she actually wanted to *have fun* for once in her life.

"Have you taught others?"

"I've tried to get Mercy to go out there. But she's nervous. And she thinks the water's too cold."

"Won't it be too cold, now?"

"We could do it sooner than later. If we go this month and stick to midday, it won't be too bad."

"Tomorrow?" Clara asked, finding in herself a degree of courage that she didn't know she had. The kind of courage that came from a genuine, unadulterated *crush*.

Then again, weren't crushes usually one way?

Jake squeezed her hands and answered, "I guess we've planned our second date, then."

CHAPTER 18—AMELIA

Amelia sat at Clara's vanity, staring at the gun, unable to touch it.

She'd always wondered what had happened after that day in Mr. Carmichael's office; she never did see or hear of the gun again. Not from her parents. Not from school. Not even her drama friends wanted to talk about it.

In his office, the principal had droned on about how hard it must have been to try to fit in in that day and age. He talked about how he'd been privy to the rumors swirling around Amelia's sister. He knew things could be tough. So, before dismissing her back to class, he drew his finger to his lips and told her that it could be their little secret. He'd do her that favor.

When she frowned at him and asked *why*, he simply said, "I owe it to your family, let's just say."

At that point, Amelia assumed that he was referring, perhaps, to some old Birch Harbor grudge. That was a "thing" in town. Old family grudges—*who* had claim to *what* property and *when* that claim had begun. That was a popular one.

But she didn't dare ask him to explain further. She didn't dare ask her parents about any of it. She simply accepted the favor and, over time, lost the event to the annals of her memory.

After all, her life changed in other ways in the months after that little drama. There was a baby in the house. Kate soon left for college. Amelia was looked over for roles in the subsequent school musicals, and life, well, just went on.

But as she now sat staring at that heavy chunk of metal, she recalled the reading of Nora's will. Of course, when Michael had declared that Amelia would get the gun, she couldn't speak up. He was a *lawyer* for goodness' sake. He could have her arrested. *It was HIS gun.* What was the statute of limitations on stealing a gun? Probably didn't even exist. You could probably never get away with that sort of crime, no matter how innocent you really were.

Then after the reading, when she had moments with her sisters to share the truth, she realized there was nothing much to share. Her friend took Michael's gun. She tried to cover it up. Things got lost in the chaos, and she stupidly kept mum for years.

And then even later, when she learned about Gene Carmichael, everything fit together.

But still, Amelia couldn't say a thing.

Confessing to the story still carried a threat. That her boyfriend would find out. And how could Michael see past a teenage error of that magnitude? What if he couldn't? Then her only hope at true love would slip like grains of sand through her fingers.

But now she had new information. The gun wasn't stowed in a bottom drawer somewhere with a collection of whoopie cushions, contraband cigarettes, maybe a half-drunk bottle of scotch, or whatever high school principals snuck between meetings with parents.

Or at least, not anymore—if it ever was.

If Carmichael *didn't* keep her secret and perhaps told Amelia's parents after all, then how come Nora and Wendell never said anything?

And if he *did* keep her secret, how had the gun made its way back to Nora?

Amelia blinked. Maybe it wasn't the same gun.

She considered calling Kate but thought better of it. Kate would judge her. Criticize her. Kate would dredge up the past.

Clara was on a date, but she was too young to understand anyway.

Only Megan would get it. Megan, who also had a flair for the rebellious and a repulsion for holding the past against the present.

"LET ME GET THIS STRAIGHT," Megan said. The three of them —Amelia, Megan, and Brian—now sat in Clara's living room, the gun pointing in the opposite direction as it lay on its side on the coffee table. "You were at a party at Michael's house back in the nineties. Your friend found this thing," Megan gestured to the piece, "and Michael walked in, so you shoved it down your pants *instead* of saying, 'Hi, we found this. Sorry?'"

"You're not thinking like a teenager," Amelia protested, aggravated. She never should have called Megan. "I was a *teenager*," she pressed.

"You weren't an *idiot*," Megan shot back, shaking her head. "But it's been forever, Amelia. Just call Michael. Get it over with. He won't care by now. His father is dead. And anyway, it's just a gun."

"Wait a minute," Brian cut in. "Does this mean Wendell never had a gun?" He was still playing catch up. Megan had mentioned the will to him, and Amelia recalled it aloud there in the living room, before she revealed her discovery, as a way to offer some context.

Megan's voice fell to a murmur, "I've been wondering about that, too, you know."

"I don't know if he had a gun. I was suspicious when Michael read the will, but you can see how my hands were tied."

"They weren't tied, Amelia," Megan replied. "And they aren't tied now. You and Michael are both grown adults. I think you can handle a misunderstanding. Or whatever this is."

Amelia let out a sigh. She *prayed* they could handle a misunderstanding. She and Michael hadn't had their first hardship yet. "This will be our first argument."

"How do you know it will be an argument?" Brian asked.

Shrugging, Amelia focused on the gun. "I don't know, I guess. I'm *assuming*." she answered. And maybe it wouldn't be an argument. But she wasn't willing to upset what they had. What they had was too delicate. Too perfect.

"So, you're just going to hide it again? Forever? Keep this little secret from him?" Megan proposed sardonically.

Her little sister made a good point. If Amelia kept mum, she wasn't only lying by omission, but she would also have to lie outright when he asked her what she'd found in that stupid drawer. If she fibbed and said she'd found her father's gun, for example, he'd want to see it. It could inform them on the case, after all. Then what would she do? She threw up her hands. "Yeah. I don't know."

"Tell him, Amelia. You're making this a way bigger deal than it really is. You were just a kid. You made a stupid mistake."

Brian added, "Maybe the gun was something special, and he'd be happy to have it back. You know, sentimental value?"

Amelia groaned. "I *hope* it wasn't special, *geez*."

Megan waved her husband off. "It doesn't matter if it was special or not." Then she grabbed Amelia's hand and stared hard at her. "Call him. Take the gun to his house. Get it over with. And," she added, dropping her voice, "if you two really are meant to be together, then this whole thing will push you closer to that. Not farther away. I *promise*."

Something deep down told Amelia that Megan knew what she was talking about. And anyway, the whole situation really was like a play—and a good play needed conflict. She and Michael had no conflict. Maybe this would *improve* their storyline.

The grandfather clock came into Amelia's focus. "Oh my gosh—you both have to go. *I* have to go. It's going to be two hours soon."

"Two hours? What do you mean?" Megan asked, her face scrunching in confusion.

Amelia dragged her up by the arm and waved them toward the door. "Clara's *date*. She told me to scram within two hours. Just in case."

"In case what?" Brian asked over his shoulder.

Amelia grabbed the gun from the table and her purse from the kitchen bar and followed them out.

"In case everything goes well," she replied, locking the door behind her.

Once Megan and Brian were in their SUV, their brake lights glowing as they rolled down toward town, Amelia buckled her seatbelt and took her phone out. With fear in her mind and hope in her heart, she called Michael.

He answered after one ring.

"Michael, hi." She squeezed her eyes shut and tried to lighten her tone. "How are you?"

It didn't work.

"Amelia? Is everything okay? You sound weird."

"Everything is *fine*," she tried for cheeriness, but it came out falsetto and awkward, and she knew she couldn't. Not now. Not before rehearsing. "I just—" She swallowed, searching for some version of the truth that would buy her time.

"Are you all right?" he asked. Maybe he wasn't the enemy. Maybe he was a soft landing for all her fears.

Amelia let out a breath and stared blankly at the night beyond her windshield. "I'm fine. It's just... it's the drawer. I opened it. And, well, do you remember my mother's will?"

Of course he did. He helped her write it. He referenced every step of their investigation, like it was a road map to finding her dad.

"Did you find Wendell's *gun*?"

She closed her eyes and sucked in as much air as her lungs could hold. "Not exactly."

CHAPTER 19—KATE

Breakfast at the Inn. Nine a.m. sharp. BYO gossip ;)

Kate loved having her sisters back in town. Even if it meant things were getting a little muddy here and there. But that's what emergency text messages were for.

The women had to stay on top of each other's good news and bad, and even Kate needed to vent a little. Of course, ultimately, she decided to preserve Matt and Vivi's honor by letting her own sensitivities die off with the fact that Vivi's snide comment was little more than teen girl drama. Still, Kate relished another chance to speak freely.

And a woman could always speak freely with her best friends. In Kate's case, her sisters.

By ten after nine, each of the four women was present, accounted for, and cradling a coffee on the back deck.

Bacon and eggs sat at the ready in the center of the table —a second batch of breakfast, since Kate's two parties had taken theirs at seven before heading out to the water.

"Do you ever feel like you're living in a motel?" Megan asked, blowing the steam off the top of her mug.

Kate laughed. "A motel? No. Do *you*?" She lifted an eyebrow, but Megan stared off into the middle distance.

"Yes," she replied, then broke into a smile. "The Bungalows does have that feel to it. But you know what? I sort of don't mind. I think I'll look back on our time there with fondness, you know?"

Kate nodded and took a sip. "I do. It'll be a good memory. The time you started fresh."

"Speaking of which, Megan, how's everything going with the fall matchmaking event?" Clara asked.

"Why? Was your date last night *that* bad?" Megan answered, but the former flushed bright red and ducked behind her drink.

"No way," she answered.

"Clara, you have to divulge. How did it go last night?" Kate leaned in, excited.

"I'm *not* going into every last detail," Clara replied. "But let's just say he kissed me on my doorstep and disappeared into the evening like a knight."

Kate propped her chin in hand. "Aww."

"That's it?" Amelia cocked an eyebrow.

"That's *perfect*," Megan gushed.

Clara beamed back at them but then shook her head. "Okay, enough of that. Back to the drama."

Amelia held up a hand. "Fine. I'll start."

Kate's gaze narrowed on Amelia. She exchanged a look with Megan, who was obviously in on something. "What's the 'bad stuff?'"

"So, you *are* going to talk about it?" Megan asked Amelia.

"Talk about what?" Kate pried.

Amelia let out a dramatic sigh. "I found 'dad's' gun last night." She made air quotes with her fingers and threw a pointed look at Clara.

"Oh, I forgot about the drawer," Clara half-murmured. "You weren't there when I got in—"

"You told me to leave within two hours," Amelia replied.

"Two hours of what? What *drawer*?" Kate asked, stealing a slice of bacon and crunching into it.

"You tell them," Amelia threw her head toward the water, and Kate had no idea what was going on. But Megan apparently did because she was the one who replied.

"No, this is *your* business. *You* tell them." Then Megan turned to the others. "It is *not* a big deal. In fact, it's such a small thing, that you will all laugh and promptly move on to more important news, like the fact that Brian and I came up with an amazing idea for the field *and* the business."

"Ooh," Clara interjected. "That's exciting."

"Fine!" Amelia cried out. "Fine, I'll tell."

Kate and Clara shook heads at each other, grinning, and then Amelia launched into an explanation of an event that happened so long ago, and for so petty a reason, that Kate nearly fell asleep mid coffee sip.

"So now," Amelia finished, "I have to confess all this to Michael, and if he breaks up with me, then my life is over."

"Wow." Megan was the first to speak after Amelia. "You've turned a whole lot of nothing into a big pot of something, haven't you? I mean—you're even worse off than you were last night."

"Let me get this straight," Clara chimed in. "What you found in that top drawer was Michael's *dad's* gun. That you 'accidentally' stole back in high school. And Mr. Carmichael confiscated it. But it somehow wound back up with Mom? And she never spoke of it?"

During Clara's review of the facts, Kate grew more interested. "I'll admit it's weird that Mom never said anything. Was there a note or anything to go with the gun?"

Amelia shook her head miserably.

"The best I would guess," Megan answered, "is that Gene figured it belonged to Dad and gave it to Mom at some point."

"But why wouldn't she say anything?" Kate reiterated. "It's an easy conversation."

"Not for Mom," Clara pointed out. "She was always worried someone was going to dig up her skeletons and hang them on the laundry line for all to see. It makes perfect sense, actually. She probably figured that if Amelia was keeping the secret, then she'd better, too."

"And Megan's right," Kate added. "Michael won't be that mad, Amelia. You're not kids anymore."

"Well, I have another question," Clara said. "Could he already know?"

"Already know that I stole his dad's gun and never said anything about it?" Amelia asked.

"Surely his dad noticed that it was gone back then and made an issue of it. Maybe his dad even accused him."

Amelia seemed to consider Clara's point and frowned. "Yeah. I see what you mean. But then it's really awkward." Her eyes flashed up. "Wait a minute. What if the *only* reason he's dating me is because he *knows* I've had the gun all these years, and he's waiting for me to break? Waiting to have the gun returned. What if our entire relationship is a *lie*?"

"Oh my God," Kate moaned and leaned forward to refresh her coffee. "This is ridiculous."

"Moving on," Megan added.

But Clara held up her hand. "You're afraid." She narrowed her gaze on Amelia. Kate and Megan kept mum.

Amelia nodded. "I'm scared to death he's going to break up with me."

"Then why are you with him?" Clara replied. "What fun is dating someone if your relationship is this fragile?"

Megan joined in now. "I don't think their relationship *is* this fragile," she said. "I think Amelia is too scared of conflict to even know *what* kind of relationship they have."

Amelia looked down, and Kate assumed a pout session was about to commence.

But she was wrong.

"You're right," Amelia replied. "I've never..." She blinked and looked out at the water. "I've never *cared* about a man this much." Her eyes turned wet, and she swiped a finger beneath each. "I don't want to threaten what we have."

"Amelia," Kate reasoned softly, "if you can't be honest with him, then you *are* threatening what you have."

Amelia sighed and plucked a strip of bacon from the platter. "You know what? You're right." She broke the slice into two and played with them for a moment. "We're getting together after this." Her eyes moved up to meet Kate's. "I'm going to come clean."

"Don't make it a bigger deal than it is," Megan cautioned.

"Don't hold back," Clara added.

Kate propped her elbows on the table. "Don't listen to them," she told Amelia, holding her sister's gaze. "Just tell the truth, apologize, and tell him how you feel."

"That I love him," Amelia added quietly.

"Yes. That and that you don't need him," Kate added.

Amelia frowned. "What?"

"You and Michael have been this crime-fighting duo for the entirety of your relationship. A relationship that was founded on the fact that you said you needed help to track down our father, right?"

"Well, it *started* that way, but so what?"

Kate rested her hand on Amelia's. "Michael needs to know that you don't need him for that. He needs to know that you're over Dad. That whatever happened to him—and whether or not we ever find out—is irrelevant to your relationship."

Kate could see Amelia swallow the advice, run it through her brain, and after some moments, she nodded. "Okay. I think that's true. I think you're right, but isn't that a lot to tack on to the gun admission?"

Smiling, she squeezed Amelia's hand. "They go together, don't they? Two truths?" Amelia shrugged, but Kate went on, "You can do it. And no matter what, you have us, right?"

Clara added, "And you have that amazing lighthouse, don't forget."

Megan joined in, too, "And apparently, you have my daughter, who seems to prefer you over me anyway." She laughed, but the other three turned to her.

"Sounds like it's Megan's turn?" Amelia said, grinning.

Kate smiled, too. She realized she didn't even need to talk about her worries over Vivi or the fact that the attic reno was taking too long or any other little trouble in her life. What fed Kate's soul wasn't being the center of attention or having her own problems solved. What fed her soul was having the chance to help solve her sisters' problems. To cry with them. To laugh with them. Celebrate and mourn and do all the things that were stolen from them when Kate stole their innocence so many years ago.

"Well," Megan answered, cutting through Kate's thoughts. "We're about to win Sarah back, in fact." She wriggled her eyebrows and laughed.

"What does that mean?" Amelia asked through a mouthful of bacon.

"Brian and I are letting her have the field for her friends' parties," Megan announced, throwing her hair off her shoulders.

Kate frowned. "You're... what?"

"We're letting them get together on the field. When we don't have an event planned, of course. It's safer than the shoreline, and it won't be a secret party." She dipped her chin to Kate, who nearly choked from the implication.

"True," Kate admitted, her mind flashing back to high school and Matt and the private moments they never should have had. The ones that turned her from a doe-eyed girl into a lovestruck woman. The ones that turned her into a daughterless mother and an outcast in her own family. She swallowed and, instead of growing defensive, recognized that Megan was onto something.

"That sounds like a smart idea," Clara added.

Amelia agreed through a murmur.

"Speaking of your events," Kate went on, "what have you decided to name the fall one? And are you two still collaborating?" Kate pointed from Amelia to Megan.

Megan nodded. "Yes, actually. And, for the fall event, we're not even using the field at all. Too much construction, first of all. And we had a better location in mind."

"Where?" Clara asked.

Kate saw Megan glance at Amelia through the corner of her eye before replying, "We thought we could do it at the lighthouse?"

"My grand opening?" Amelia answered immediately, her eyes wide.

"No," Megan answered. "We'll do it the weekend before. It'll drum up attention, and it can be a dress rehearsal for you, so to speak."

Amelia's mouth cracked into a smile. "That'd be amazing. What are you going to call it?"

"Easy," Megan replied, crossing her arms and leaning back. "*Love at the Lake*."

CHAPTER 20—CLARA

With Amelia's problem addressed and Megan's new idea validated, Clara turned to Kate. "How about you? Anything new in the life of the de facto Hannigan matriarch?"

The others laughed, but Kate glowed. "I like that," she replied. "I'll be the matriarch, sure. And to answer your question, not really. I suppose I've become the boring one."

"You were always the boring one," Megan teased.

"Not always," Amelia said. "I mean, she did get pregnant in high school, after all."

"True." Megan tipped the rim of her water glass to Kate.

Clara pressed on. "Everything's going well with Matt?" Then she lowered her voice. "And Vivi?"

Megan choked beside her, sputtering on her sip of water.

"Are you okay?" Clara asked, patting her sister's back.

Nodding, she answered through coughs, "Fine. Fine. Wrong pipe."

"Matt is *great*," Kate answered. "Vivi is okay, too. There are growing pains. You know. Exactly what you might expect."

Clara nodded. "She's a complicated child, I think."

"Every child is complicated," Megan said, recovering at last from her fit. All eyes turned on her.

Amelia spoke next, "Is this about the Sarah thing?"

"What Sarah thing?" Megan shot back.

Clara winced. Even at school, she'd caught her niece squeezing down the hallway, an injured puppy among jumping, barking hounds. It was a marked difference from the summer. An alarming one. But it wasn't Clara's place to sound the alarms. And anyway, Sarah had gone out the night before. Maybe things were settling in for her?

"Sarah eating lunch in the bathroom, remember?" Amelia replied, looking at the others for back up. "I think we were all a little shocked and traumatized to hear that."

"Oh," Megan seemed to relax. "No. I mean yes, but... she went to that party last night. With Vivi and Mercy. Paige and Chloe, too. And I think it went well. Well enough that she was still snoring when I left the apartment. She stayed for the whole thing."

Clara glanced from Amelia back to Megan. "Is she living at the apartment full-time now? What happened to the arrangement with Amelia?"

"She sort of flits between us, but during the week, she's home," Megan replied.

"Most weekends, too. I guess she's getting tired of me." Amelia winked at Clara, and the tensions instantly settled.

Kate shifted in her seat. "*Actually*," she drew their attention back to her, "Matt and Vivi and I are doing as well as can be expected. I have a new game plan, and I think it'll help us bond a little."

"What's that?" Clara asked.

"I think I'm going to tell her about what happened," Kate said slowly, unevenly.

Megan jumped in, "Do you mean you're going to tell her about *Clara*?"

Clara's jaw fell open. She was already in a sensitive situation with Vivi and all the other girls at the high school. "No," she spat.

Kate turned to her, concern filling her eyes. "What?"

"You can't, Kate. It'll ruin everything."

"Ruin what?" Amelia asked.

Megan held a hand up. "Actually—"

"No," Clara interrupted her, leaning forward and pressing her palms on the table. "Kate, please. If Vivi knows that I'm technically her half-sister, she'll make my life a living hell at school. We finally warmed up to each other on Friday. You can't." Clara swallowed and looked at each sister in turn. "Right?"

Amelia nodded. "Leave it alone, Kate. As far as this town knows, Clara *is* our sister. Her students should see it that way, too. God forbid such a thing get back to old Judith Carmichael."

Kate frowned but nodded. "Okay."

But when Clara looked at Megan, she didn't see the same promise. "Megan? Swear to me you'll make sure Sarah doesn't tell."

Megan chewed her lower lip for a moment too long but finally said, "Yeah. I'll talk to Sarah about it."

AFTER BREAKFAST WITH HER SISTERS, Clara slipped into the upstairs bath to get changed for her diving lesson with Jake.

The others had teased her only momentarily before each wandered away to her own personal business. Amelia to Michael's house to talk about the gun. Megan to the apartment to talk to Sarah, hopefully. And Kate to turn rooms and clean the kitchen before the afternoon check-ins.

Clara owned exactly one bathing suit, and it would have to do. She hadn't donned it for a date *ever*, but she wore it that summer and felt good enough. It was conservative as far as bathing suits for twenty-somethings went. A tankini, the sort her mother pushed on her. Even in her slight build, the top fit snugly, accentuating her minimal curves and turning her from premature schoolmarm to normal, nicely developed twenty-eight-year-old.

She pulled on a peach cover-up and slid her feet into a pair of teetering wedges before taking to her hair, drawing the top half into a spunky, messy bun on top of her head and leaving the rest loose around her neck. Then makeup—even without a blindfold, she'd need waterproof again, but she kept it lighter, adding just touches of mascara and a smear of lip gloss.

Studying herself in the mirror, her main concern was that she looked a little too young for Jake. But then, there wasn't much she could or would do about that. Determined to have fun for once and forgo the ever-nagging worries that her brain mixed up for her, she grabbed her black sunglasses from the desk, called goodbye to Kate, and headed straight for the marina.

As soon as she made it onto the sidewalk that cut from the house toward the Village, she spotted him, in the doorway of the marina office, chatting with whoever was inside.

From that angle, Clara had a private moment to gawk. His athletic build. His height. Tan skin and sun-kissed hair. Traits that just months ago, she'd never stopped to fully admire in a man. A late bloomer or distracted or low local inventory, whatever the cause for her delayed interest in the opposite sex—it was gone. Out the window.

She nearly chickened out, slowing to a stop where the sidewalk forked into two cobblestone paths—one to the Village and one to the marina.

"Clara Hannigan, isn't it?"

The voice came from the first path—the Birch Village one.

Swallowing, Clara turned her head. Walking straight toward her was a vaguely familiar woman. Short, icy blonde hair. A crisp white button-down. Blood-red linen shorts that hit too high on her thin, vascular thighs, which gave way to knobby knees, veiny shins, and strappy sandals. Across her arm was an oversized wicker tote. She pulled trendy tortoiseshell glasses down off her nose and pointed at Clara with them. "Yes, Clara. Hello."

The greeting fell somewhere between snotty and sweet, and Clara froze momentarily before flicking a nervous glance toward Jake and the office. He hadn't seen her yet, but he was now dragging heavy-looking cannisters from the office. Prepping for their date, no doubt. Oblivious to Clara's internal scream for help.

But Clara was an adult. Capable. Strong.

She returned her attention to the woman. "Mrs. Carmichael. Hello."

CHAPTER 21—MEGAN

When she returned to the apartment, Brian was reading the newspaper at the breakfast bar, and Sarah was tucked into the corner of the sofa with her phone. A glass of OJ sat on the side table.

Megan hated to disrupt such a serene moment.

"Hey, you two," she began, setting her keys down and strolling to the sofa.

Brian murmured good morning. Sarah glanced up briefly with a small, tired smile.

Megan caught her husband's attention from over their daughter's head, gave him the look, and jutted her chin toward the door.

At first, he frowned but then got the hint, shuffling the newspaper together and standing up noisily. "I'm meeting Matt at the field to talk about a few things. I'd better get going."

She rolled her eyes at his obviousness but couldn't suppress a grin before lowering onto the sofa, a full cushion length away from Sarah.

She grabbed the remote and clicked the TV on.

"Nothing good on Sunday mornings," Sarah commented, standing and moving to the kitchen.

"Want me to make you some breakfast?" Megan tried.

From the pantry, Sarah waved a sleeve of bagels. "I'm good."

Megan nodded and pulled her own phone to her face, scrolling mindlessly, waiting for the right moment.

"Where were you this morning?" Sarah asked, popping her bagel into the toaster and pulling cream cheese from the fridge.

"Oh, me?" Megan settled deeper into the sofa. "Breakfast at Kate's. I didn't want to wake you."

"Thanks," Sarah answered, her tone even and cool. Normal.

"So, how did it go last night?"

"How did what go?" The toaster dinged, and Sarah popped the bagel out.

Megan feigned a yawn. "The party. The beach party, or whatever."

"Oh, it was actually *really* fun," Sarah replied, bringing her breakfast to the sofa and sinking back into her spot. Megan held back from gushing. Not only had Sarah *enjoyed* herself with friends, but she was also willing to talk about it? This was going well. Very well.

Carefully, Megan took some moments to browse channels before replying. Finally, she settled on a *Golden Girls* rerun and set the remote down. "So, what do you do at a beach party, exactly?"

"Oh, you know," Sarah responded through a mouthful. "Just walked along the beach and talked, mostly. We made another bonfire, but some adult came by and said they were going to call the police because we didn't have a permit or something, so we had to put it out. Vivi told them that

Mercy's dad was in charge of the lake, though, so then the adult sort of just got mad and stomped off. It was kind of funny."

Megan lifted an eyebrow. "Vivi is... a *confident* girl. That's for sure."

"Yeah, and she's already crazy popular. Especially for being a freshman. Which is weird, because this summer, she acted like *I* was her ticket to fame or something." Sarah glanced at her mom and shrugged. "Turns out I never cared about that to begin with. And it turns out she didn't need me anyway."

"I'm glad," Megan answered. "Being popular is overrated, you know." Inside, Megan was brimming with the joy of having such an easy, open conversation with Sarah. But she knew that it was a delicate dance. If she spoke too much... asked *too* many questions, the conversation would die. And, of course, she couldn't be totally indifferent. "What's Mercy like? She seems... quiet?"

"Mercy is crazy smart and super sweet. Young, though. She gets really wigged out sometimes. Like nervous and stuff."

"About what?"

"Literally everything." Sarah took a sip of her juice. "I think being friends with Vivi scares her or something."

"Vivi kind of scares me," Megan admitted, lifting her eyebrow at Sarah, who smiled sympathetically.

"She's all talk. She's, like, a *wannabe* mean girl, but her dad is super strict, so she doesn't get far with it."

Megan let out a sigh. The truth was taking shape. The reason Vivi sidled up with Sarah to begin with—an older alliance who could help loosen Matt up, perhaps? But then—

"So Sarah, about Vivi—"

"Listen, Mom. If you're going to ask about Vivi and the big secret—" Sarah warned, but Megan started to shake her head and hold her hands up. Sarah went on, "Because I can't *make* her forget that, Mom."

"Right. I know. But Clara is worried that Vivi is going to... I don't know... *use it against her* at school or something. You know Clara has Vivi and Mercy in her class."

"I know, and I can't control that."

"But you can set a good example for her. Right?"

"I can't control Vivi. And I'm not even technically *friends* with her."

"So, you didn't hang out with her last night?"

"I hung out with everyone last night, Mom. It was a party. That's how parties go. You sort of hang out with everyone."

"You know, Aunt Kate wants to tell Vivi about Clara. Clear the air." She was talking to her daughter as though they were on the same plane now. That's how it went when there was a secret hanging in the balance. The two secret holders were instantly and unavoidably on the same level. There was no getting around it. Even if they were mother and daughter. Even if there was a twenty-something-year age difference.

"Why don't you just tell Clara that Vivi knows?" Sarah asked.

It was an entirely reasonable question. And Megan *should* be able to do that. "But," she started, "I don't think Clara cares if Vivi knows as much as if the entire school knows. You know? And as far as she believes, *nobody* knows. It's keeping her sane while she adjusts to the new school."

Sarah's face twisted in confusion. "If I were her, I'd care more about *Vivi* knowing. But since she already does... what difference does it make?"

"What's that supposed to mean? You think Vivi *will* use it against her?" Megan asked.

Sarah shrugged. "I think Vivi is a loose cannon."

"Good expression," Megan complimented. "And she does seem that way. Maybe she just needs a distraction. Like a club or something. You know? Or a boyfriend?" Megan knew she sounded like a teenager herself, but she also knew that when young girls concocted evil plans—or when they had the propensity to—it was time for a project.

"She's doing cheerleading," Sarah replied. "And the boys are already in love with her."

"Does she like any of them back? Maybe she needs help making something happen."

Sarah rolled her eyes. "*Mom*, high school isn't the real world. We don't need *matchmakers*. And anyway, she doesn't like high school guys."

"What do you mean?" Megan asked, frowning.

Sarah made a face, wadded the rest of her bagel in her paper towel, and twisted in her seat. "She likes *older* guys."

CHAPTER 22—AMELIA

On the phone the evening prior, Amelia and Michael had made plans to meet for breakfast before their writing session for the re-enactment. Typically, Michael came to Amelia. To the lighthouse. But this time, she needed to be the one to go to him.

So there they were, in his house in Harbor Hills. The one with the flowerpots and the mailbox—where she'd had a chance to deposit the gun like a misguided thief who second-guessed her bad choices.

When she arrived, she felt like a kid all over again, walking up the brick path and ringing his doorbell, her boho bag held tightly against her hip.

He was there in a second, ready, waiting, and anxious to help her with her father's search and learn more about the locked drawer and the gun inside—the one he didn't know belonged to *him*.

What he didn't know was that her revelation wouldn't help the search. More likely, it would derail it.

In fact, it might push their relationship further away than ever before.

Michael greeted her with a peck on the cheek and waved her toward his kitchen. "Come on in." He was dressed leisurely, in sweats and a black tee that clung to the muscles in his back and made her second guess everything she was about to do.

"Coffee?"

"Sure," she replied, hooking the handles of her bag on the back of a barstool and sliding onto it. "How was your night? Did you get any work done?"

"Ugh," he groaned. "Yes and no. The whole Island case is a mess. I don't know exactly how it will pan out, but St. Mary's needs to just expand back into a high school."

"Why did they close that part, anyway? Too few students to keep it open?"

"Actually," Michael answered, placing a steaming mug in front of her. "That's something I wanted to investigate."

Her heartrate slowed. It wasn't a bad thing that Michael had been hired for something contentious and time consuming. It was a nice diversion to remind both of them that the world was bigger than what happened to Wendell Acton.

"Are you representing St. Mary's or the families? Or who? I'm a little confused about this whole thing," Amelia replied, happy to ease into her own revelation on the heels of someone else's drama.

"I'm representing the families who wish to bring a suit against Birch Harbor Unified."

Amelia's heart sank a little. "Really? You're siding with the people who want to sue the school district?"

"What?" he replied. "It's not personal, Amelia. It's nothing against Clara. Or even the school. It's just a matter of offering a local school option to the Island kids."

Shrugging, she felt uneasy all over again. "So, what is it you want to investigate?"

"Well," he took a sip of his coffee and winced, "Too hot. Anyway, we know that St. Mary's went through three iterations. Way back, years ago. First, they offered grades kindergarten through eight and had two campuses. The boys' building and the girls'. Both 'schools' on the campus served Catholic families only and kept the students strictly separated. Then, before it became co-ed and they took in any denomination, they added the high school. *But*, they only added the high school for a short time and only allowed girls. Your mom's yearbook is proof of that. But the weird thing about the yearbook is how few girls there were *and*—" He reached to the far end of the bar and pulled the familiar hardback down to her.

"Hey," Amelia cut in. "You *took* this from my place?"

"No, no." Michael chuckled. "I checked out my own copy from the special collections at the library. I was looking for something else when I decided to see what they had from St. Mary's, too. And, voila."

"They don't check out special collections material."

"They do to lawyers and historians," he replied, grinning. "Which you're about to become too, remember?"

A grin shaped her mouth, and she flipped the book open, marveling all over again at the hairdos of the past. The black and white photos of young women in church and at the Village, sipping malts. "You were saying?" she asked as she turned the pages.

"So, if you really go through this thing," he pointed at it, "you'll note that there are only two pages of student portraits, and each page is technically just a half page. The pictures are big, right? Each girl with her own mini bio. Even Judith Banks."

Amelia flipped back to the portraits and studied Judith. Her face was almost pain-stricken. Then again, so was Nora's. No sign of a giggly teenage girl. Just severe expressions beneath beehives of hair. It now appeared that Nora and Judith had known each other long before Gene Carmichael entered the picture.

Or had they? When *had* Nora met Gene, exactly? When had Judith, for that matter? And did it even matter at all?

When Clara had initially brought to Amelia's attention the revelation that Nora and Judith went to school together, it was jarring.

But over the past week, it fell away, like a boring, bland little truth nugget that meant nothing. It made perfect sense that the women knew each other, especially if Judith grew up out on Heirloom. What didn't make sense was why Nora's daughters were left in the dark about it. The only logical answer was that the islanders kept their distance back in those days. Back then, the division between Heirloom and Birch Harbor was sharp as a razor. And if Nora had a beef with any one specific person, she'd have covered it up. Protecting her image was a priority, after all.

Amelia bristled with her inability to see what any of it had to do with anything. Plus, she still hadn't addressed the gun in her tote.

"So what?" Amelia answered. "So what if there aren't many students? It was a Catholic school for girls. I'd be surprised if there were more."

"Fair point," Michael acknowledged. "But then take a look at some of the names, Amelia." He pressed a finger to a line of women. "Do any of these names look familiar to you?"

Amelia shrugged. "No? But this was way before I was even born. Of course I wouldn't know them."

"We *should* know them. If Nora went to school there, then other Birch Harbor folks must have, too, right? Or, by a different logic, Heirloom Island people must have made their way inland eventually. This town is way too small for only *two* of these girls to be familiar to us. Where are the Matuszewskis? Other Hannigans? Bankses? Van Holts? Fiorillos?"

Again, Amelia came up empty. "I don't know," she answered. Thoughts of the gun reared back to life, and she was losing interest in his spiel. They had bigger fish to fry, no doubt. She opened her mouth to say so, but he went on.

"So I cross-referenced the names from your mother's yearbook and—" he pulled another stack of books down the bar, "—St. Mary's' earlier yearbooks. They kept books for kinder through eighth grade, both the girls' school and the boys', but I focused on the girls first, of course."

"Okay." Amelia flipped the book on top open. It was thin, too.

"Amelia," Michael rested his hand on hers, stilling it and staring into her eyes. "Your mother didn't *go* to St. Mary's until high school."

Amelia frowned. "I know," she said at last. "She went to Birch Harbor until eighth then transferred to St. Mary's in ninth. Or tenth grade, maybe. I don't really remember. But so what, Michael?"

"Why did she transfer?" he asked, his expression hardened.

Shrugging, Amelia took a long sip of her coffee. "Because her parents were Catholic. Devout, in fact. And so was Mom."

He grabbed another of the books in the stack and pointed at its cover. *Birch Harbor High. Class of '54.* Birch Harbor *High.* She lifted her eyebrow at him. He flipped it open to a page he'd bookmarked with a sticky note. Again, he pointed, this time to a black-and-white photo.

"Aunt Rose," Amelia murmured. She wouldn't have recognized the woman, whom she'd only met once or twice as a child, if not for the fact that her name read clear as day beneath her photograph. *Rose Hannigan.*

Michael repeated the same action again with yet another book from his stack, pointing eventually to another woman. Amelia frowned then pulled the glossy pages toward her, flipping back to the cover. *Birch Harbor High. Class of '61.* Aunt Roberta was immediately familiar even before Amelia's eyes flitted down to her printed name. *Roberta Hannigan.* The one who moved to Arizona and stayed there. The one who took them in the summer before Clara was born.

But recognizing Roberta and knowing of Rose didn't help Amelia understand Michael's point. "I don't get it," she finally confessed, throwing her hands up.

"Birch Harbor High, Amelia. These two Hannigans went to Birch Harbor High from ninth until twelfth grade. And so did your mom's brothers, too. They're in here." He stabbed down at the stack of books. "Birch Harbor *High.*"

"But my mom didn't go to Birch Harbor High. She went to St. Mary's." Amelia frowned and gently closed the yearbook before looking at Michael. "Nora was the only one in her family who went to St. Mary's instead."

Michael nodded seriously. "Exactly. And I called St. Mary's and inquired about the time period during which they had the high school open and running. I did some math, but *nothing* adds up, Amelia."

"What does this have to do with the lawsuit, though?" Her brows remained furrowed as she drank from her mug.

"That's where our two interests merge, Amelia." He held

both of her hands and stared at her. "At first, I figured I could find out if St. Mary's has the capacity to add a high school. If they do, then no one needs to sue anyone else. I'd be happy to help facilitate the reopening of a second building. I mean, come on. I'm Catholic, too. It'd do the Island good. Plus, Birch Harbor Unified can squirrel away their funding and not crack into the logistics of taxing the Island and dragging the kids over. Everyone is happy, right?"

"Well, do they? Have the capacity, I mean?"

He shook his head. "That's just it. It's not even close. The school operates almost strictly from two funding sources: tuition and donations. They get no public money from the state or any locality, of course. And they scholarship a large proportion of their students."

"But opening a new high school will draw in more money. More tuition and donations, right?"

"When I talked to Father Bart, he told me that the only reason they ever even offered the secondary grades—the high school classes—was because of 'the *times*.'"

"The *times*? More people were religious back then. Devout, no doubt?" Amelia asked.

But Michael shook his head. "They may have been more religious, yes. But that wasn't what he meant."

Amelia pulled her hands away and pushed her fingertips into the corners of her eyes, rubbing and frowning. She wasn't enough of a critical thinker for any of their conversation. At last, exasperated by being held hostage by the fact that she still needed to talk about the gun, she forced a smile and propped her chin in her hand. "I give up, Michael. What did Father Bart mean? What does *all* of this mean?" She passed her free hand across the mess of dusty yearbooks.

Michael lowered his face to the table, holding her gaze.

"Judith Carmichael, Nora Hannigan, and the rest of the unfamiliar girls didn't *go* to St. Mary's." He dropped his voice another octave, and his face grew closer to hers. "They were *sent* there."

CHAPTER 23—KATE

Once her sisters left to see to their Sunday errands, Kate began cleaning. It was her therapy —scrubbing the sink basin until it squeaked, sweeping table crumbs into her hand and replacing them with a fresh candle. Rubbing oil into the wooden fixtures of her little business. Her home.

Saturday guests would be checking out soon, but a couple of hours remained until Sunday check-in. Over the course of the summer, Sunday had proved to be the second slowest day of the week. Many guests opted to stay through to Monday—three-day weekends were all the rage on Lake Huron. More often than not, however, most needed to return to work come Monday.

No one had booked for that night, but in the past couple of months, Kate quickly learned that meant rather little in Birch Harbor. It wasn't uncommon for day visitors to decide they rather liked the little lakeside town and might care to stay an extra day. It was next to impossible to secure an Airbnb on the spot, and the motel up off Harbor Ave. left something to be desired. Once they learned about the Heirloom Inn, charm set in, and with the snap of her fingers, Kate was booked up.

Now, as she dragged her vacuum attachment down the hallway baseboard, she thought to the week ahead.

It would be Clara's second week of school. Probably harder in some ways than the first. Easier, in others. If Vivi kept the peace, then maybe things would settle in.

Megan and Amelia were hard at work on their fall plans —Megan's *Love at the Lake* and Amelia's grand opening. Kate needed to prepare her own marketing for each event. They had decided as a group to work in conjunction as much as possible, after all.

Later, Kate would call her boys to check in. See how their semester was shaping up. How their girlfriends were. If Thanksgiving plans were still a *go*.

At some point, Kate would need to run to the store, too. She had promised Matt she'd make her famous lemon chicken that night, but distraction was already taking over.

The problem with running the Inn was exactly what her sisters had warned her about. She *lived* at work.

And Kate wouldn't mind living there if she at least had some reprieve throughout the day. But hiring someone felt monumental. She'd need to scour her finances and see if such a proposition were even feasible.

If so, though, Kate did happen to have a couple of young locals in mind to man the front desk, turn rooms, and help with cleaning.

Whether they were up to the task was another question.

After she finished the hall, Kate went to find her phone. Perhaps it didn't hurt to reach out now to see if the girls she had in mind were looking for a part-time job for the fall. Maybe something to help them save up for Christmas?

"Hello?"

The voice came from the open window by the front door.

Had Kate missed the doorbell?

"Hello?" she answered, dropping her phone on the desk and moving toward the door.

As she opened it, she started to apologize... that she was *vacuuming*, you see, and she didn't hear—

"Oh." The wind flew from Kate's chest, and she had to grope for a breath when her gaze settled on the source of the greeting. "Mrs. ... *Carmichael*, is it?"

"Judith, please," the woman replied. "I hope I'm not disturbing you?"

Kate pressed the porch screen open and waved her hand back out of pure muscle memory. "No," she said, still breathless. "Come in."

"I try to keep up with local businesses, you know." Impossibly, Judith sat on Kate's very own back deck, sipping an iced tea and generally luxuriating in the discomfort that her uninvited visit had established.

"Mmm," Kate replied, perched stolidly at the edge of her seat, one eye on Judith. One on the door. Who knew what this woman had up her sleeve?

"So, you've been open since the beginning of the summer, as I understand," Judith noted, her hands now clasped on the table.

"I beg your pardon, Mrs. Carmichael," Kate interrupted, regaining some of her wherewithal at last. "But is this a common habit?"

"And what's that, dear?" she replied. Her newly assumed grandmotherly tone didn't quite strike right.

"Summer representatives of the town council popping in on local businesses in a sort of informal... *evaluation*?"

"Oh, my stars, *no*." The woman's voice shook. "This is *not* an evaluation. Hah!" A craggy edge cut across the bitter laugh, and Kate wondered if Judith had ever been a smoker. The lines along her mouth were more prominent than those on her forehead. Then again, the ones on her neck were most prominent of all. Had she had work done? Could two retired educators afford a home, a houseboat, and a few rounds of Botox? Kate thought not.

In the absence of a response from Kate, Judith filled the conversational void. "I like to support the local businesses, and so that's what I'm here to do today, Miss Hannigan. *Kate*. Or... weren't you married?"

"Widowed," Kate answered. She ignored the first part of the question and found footing to take the upper hand. "So what, then? You're here to buy a gift card?"

"Actually," Judith replied, glancing down at her drink and then out to the water. "I'd like to book a night at the Heirloom Inn."

CHAPTER 24—CLARA

After a curt exchange, Clara had continued past Mrs. Carmichael and to the marina, but not before she stole one last glance over her shoulder to watch as the woman slipped into the house on the harbor. The Inn.

Bewildered, Clara retrieved her phone from her bag to call Kate and demand to know what in the *world* was going on, but just as she was about to hit *Call*, another voice pulled her attention away.

Jake's.

"There she is," he said as he strode toward her.

Almost immediately, Clara forgot about Judith Carmichael and Kate and the Inn.

He jogged the last few yards and slipped his arms around her waist, pulling her into him. He smelled fresh—like he'd stepped out of the shower and onto the marina, and her knees turned weak.

"Hi," Clara replied, grinning, once he let go.

"Are you ready for this?"

"Ready as I'll ever be." Clara let out a sigh, her chest rising and falling as Jake grabbed her hand and guided her down to the office. Once there, the deckhand hefted one bag up, and Jake took another, falling in step behind the boy so he and Clara could walk together.

"There's a great place where we can start down near the private homes in Heirloom Cove," he told her, striding to her side. "When the instructors take students, they go up here or north toward the lighthouse. I figure that area might be a little busier since it's the weekend."

A *private* lesson in a *private* locale. Clara's skin prickled. Jake Hennings certainly knew how to ramp up the suspense.

They passed the Inn on their walk, and Clara glanced up briefly, catching sight of Kate and Mrs. Carmichael on the back porch. Kate didn't notice her.

"Do you know the Carmichaels very well?" Clara asked, nervous about derailing their date but anxious about what the woman might be doing with her sister just then.

Jake frowned and shook his head. "Not at all. I don't know many people around here, truth be told."

"But Gene Carmichael keeps his boat at the marina, right?"

"Yes. The houseboat. That's right. I see him and his wife come and go. They keep to themselves for the most part."

"What are they like?" Clara asked as Jake veered closer to the water and a chunky outcropping of rocks. The spot straddled the property line of two houses south of the Inn. No one else had set up camp there. A dock for each house drew a line on either side of their position some yards off. "Are we *allowed* to dive here?" she asked.

"Yes. The only private beach in Birch Harbor belongs to your family's house, actually." He jutted his chin back down the shore toward the Inn. Clara's insides twisted. She knew as much, but it was an easy fact to forget.

"Oh, right."

"And the folks here are part-timers. Gone for the winter. Kind of like Gene Carmichael. Which is about as much as I know. He comes down during the summer, brings his wife. They walk the town or do whatever it is they do during the day, and come back to the boat at night."

Clara refrained from carrying the conversation out any farther. No way could she allow the date to turn into a function of her family drama. No way.

Jake seemed to detect her shift. "All right," he began, dropping his bag in the sand and bending to unzip it. "First thing's first, we talk safety."

The boy set down the second bag and asked Jake if he needed more help. Jake shook his head and thanked him, and then, just like that, Clara and Jake were alone together.

She grinned and knelt next to him, helping unpack and set up as he went into great detail about how to dive, what to do, what *not* to do. Breathing seemed to be important, and Clara immediately became aware of her breaths. They turned shallow as Jake pulled his shirt off to suit up.

"We don't wear wetsuits?" Clara asked as she followed his lead, tugging her swim cover over her head and folding it into a neat square.

He shook his head and inflated the vests, then shrugged the first one onto his shoulders. "The water should be warm enough," he replied. His eyes danced down her figure. "If you're too cold, we can always go get one."

Clara shivered, but not from the cold, then shook her head. "Oh, no. It's fine. I just figured that was part of the get-up."

He grinned, waded into the water, and buckled the vest's waist strap, then the top strap. "The *get-up*. I like that."

She bit her lower lip. "Do you need help with anything?" Clara had been snorkeling. She'd been tide-pooling. She'd worn any number of life vests or jackets and even tried skiing once.

But SCUBA diving felt like a new level of water recreation.

"Your turn," Jake said.

"Maybe I should have gotten my gear on first. Now you'll have to wear that while you help me in the water," she pointed out, half-joking.

"That's what I'm here for." He grinned and directed her on what to put where, first indicating the fins. "Go ahead and put yours on." He pointed to the second set, and Clara did as he said.

"Fins but no wetsuit?" she asked and followed him into the shallow water until she, too, was waist-deep.

"The fins will make it more fun."

"I'm too inexperienced to have fun," Clara pointed out lamely.

He took her hand. "Sometimes, you have *more* fun when you're inexperienced."

Clara's breath caught in her chest, and she flushed.

"Here," Jake said, pulling her gear into the water and inflating it. "Now drop down a bit, so I can get this on you."

"Shouldn't we do this on dry land? Where it's... *safer*?"

"It's easier in the water," he said.

Clara let herself sink down. The temperature was too cold, but the blood rushing through her veins was enough of a distraction until the next one took effect—Jake within arm's reach, pulling her vest over her shoulders and organizing the tubes and straps. He kept his focus down, and Clara kept her eyes on him.

"You need to breathe," he said, his voice low as he cinched her chest strap, his eyes darting up to hers nervously.

"I can't," Clara whispered.

CHAPTER 25—AMELIA

Amelia was faced with an unnerving truth about Judith Carmichael, and—for whatever reason—just *learning* about it pushed her over the edge.

She had a play to write and produce. She had a grand opening to prepare for. Her sister's event. The ongoing and increasingly futile investigation into her father's disappearance...

But none of that held a candle to the matter that scared her the most. The gun. Her teenage error. And what it might do to the best thing she had going.

Michael.

Once he declared his suspicions about what St. Mary's *used* to be, Amelia had initially been compelled to blast off a gossipy text to her sisters.

Instead, though, she'd taken a deep breath and asked Michael if they could talk about something—just as soon as she rerouted her immediate future plans. Then, she left the kitchen and called her stage manager.

The re-enactment would be canceled, plain and simple.

With the minuscule timeframe and now her own

personal distractions, producing a full-blown show in conjunction with everything else unfolding felt utterly impossible.

And for the first time in a while, Amelia wasn't too concerned with her inability to follow through. Maybe because canceling the re-enactment felt less like a flakey decision and more like a good one. For once.

Her theater troupe wouldn't be too heartbroken, especially when she shot off a text to Megan to ask if the Birch Players could host their first annual Birch Harbor Summer Stock at the field the following summer. Megan replied immediately, agreeing easily, and the day was saved.

As Amelia paced in the front yard, her phone clutched in her two hands while she sorted through all the business, Michael waited inside. There he sat at the kitchen table, thumbing through the yearbooks and jotting notes.

When she'd handled her theater business, Amelia knew it was time to handle her personal business, too.

She re-entered the house, grabbed her bag from the barstool, her hand trembling, and slid into the seat adjacent to Michael.

He glanced up, smiling absently as he returned to his notes, his focus intense but somehow charming, like that of a nutty professor.

Amelia removed the gun from her bag and steadied her fumbling fingers enough to set it on the table, pointing away from him—out the bay window that overlooked a neat row of hedges.

He pushed his notepad away, his expression turning to a mixture of grave interest and soft confusion, cementing the image of a nutty professor.

"I'm sorry," Amelia murmured, her fingers laced on top of the table. She tried her hardest to assume a grown-up disposition. Something befitting a woman who had made mistakes long ago but now knew just how to manage her life —and the relationships that were so central to it.

"Is this—" Michael picked up the gun with care, frowning and turning it over in his hand.

Amelia swallowed. "It's... *yours*. I think."

He shook his head. "No. I don't—" He looked up at her, his eyes on fire. "This is a Smith and Wesson snub nose. Like in Nora's will. This is your *dad's*."

"No." She shook her head. "It was *your* dad's." She resisted the temptation to cover her face with her hands. "Listen, Michael. When we were kids, in high school. Do you remember that party I convinced you to host? Here?" She swept a weak arm across the kitchen.

He nodded.

"One of my drama friends found that gun somewhere in your library. Then you walked in, and I got scared, so I hid it. And then one thing led to another, and it was in my backpack, and someone told Mr. Carmichael, and he confiscated it and—"

"Wait a minute," he cut in. "This is what you found in Clara's drawer, isn't it?" He looked at her with brief wonder then returned his gaze to the gun, ignoring everything she'd just confessed.

"I'm so sorry I never told you before. I guess I figured it would make things worse, somehow. For *me*." She murmured the last two words beneath her breath.

He set the gun down and pushed his fingers through his hair, letting out a long, low breath. "The gun."

"Michael," Amelia whispered, "I'm *sorry*."

"I always *wondered* about it. And when I read Nora's will and heard about Wendell's Smith and Wesson..."

Michael glanced out the window then back to Amelia. "It wasn't my dad's," he went on. "It was my mother's."

Amelia's heart sank then and there. When he didn't say more, she asked quietly, "Your mom had a gun?"

Michael had lost his mother when she was too young. When *he* was too young, too.

He scratched his neck and then turned the heavy piece of metal in his hand, pulling the hammer back and opening the cylinder, inspecting it as if to make some confirmation. Finally, he answered her through a haze. "Her grandparents were founders, you know. She's the reason we even have this house. Had nothing to do with my dad's law practice and everything to do with her claim as a descendent of the pioneers."

Amelia knew only bits of the history behind Michael's matrilineal line. They were another of the families who first arrived in that original grove of birch trees just off Heirloom Cove.

Mila Matuszewski was born into the Van Holts. Related vaguely to the mayor. It was the Hannigans and the Van Holts who shaped Birch Harbor into what it became. At least, that was as much as Amelia knew. But she'd often heard of contentious land arguments. Differences of opinion. Banishments to the Island, even, as if the settlers were living in some Shakespearean tragedy.

"She kept a gun because she was always afraid," Michael went on.

"Afraid of what?" Amelia asked.

"That someone would come and try to take our property. You know how it was back then. Back in the earlier days, nothing was settled here. My mom was convinced that this whole area of Birch Harbor didn't actually belong to the Van Holts. She inherited it, you know."

"Inherited the house?" Amelia frowned and glanced around her. She'd never even considered the fact that the homes in the gated community of Harbor Hills were once a part of all that early controversy—the same controversy that colored Nora Hannigan and her own ancestors.

"No. She inherited the fear," Michael corrected her.

Amelia turned her head to him. "Michael, I—"

"That's why she established Harbor Hills. She did all the groundwork. Turning it into an HOA community. Drawing the boundaries. Erecting the gates." He smirked. "Stockpiling arms."

Frowning, Amelia flicked a glance to the gun then back to Michael's face. "You mean—?"

He nodded and returned the gun to the same spot Amelia had placed it initially. "She had lots of guns." He pointed to it. "I took that one from her collection and hid it for myself, actually."

Amelia blinked then flashed a look at him. "You stole it from your mom?"

"Then you stole it from me, I guess." A wry smile curled his lip, but Amelia squeezed her eyes shut and shook her head.

"Michael, I am so sorry. It was a stupid, foolish thing to do. I was young and dumb. Still am, I guess."

"How did it make its way to Nora?"

"I don't know," Amelia answered. "I just sort of figured Carmichael returned it to my parents."

"And then Nora assumed it was your dad's and left it in her will to you?" he frowned.

Amelia shrugged. "I guess?"

He crossed his arms over his chest and leaned back into his chair, studying her. Amelia felt the weight of the world converge on her heart, and she wondered if she'd made a huge error after all. If revealing her childhood dalliance *would* break them. If she'd just ruined everything.

"Did you know that my mom is the reason I agreed to have that party?"

More confused, Amelia just shook her head.

Michael went on. "Yep. She even knew about it. She was upstairs the whole time."

"And she didn't care?"

He shook his head. "My mom and your mom knew each other from the country club, Amelia. My mom sold land to your parents. The cottage."

"What do you mean the cottage?"

"That place originally belonged to my mother. It was part of this area for decades, but whoever had begun building it died mid-project. It sat in our family for a long time. Then your dad came along looking for something to purchase, and my mom all but gave it to your folks. She liked them, you know. Nora and Wendell."

Amelia frowned. "I had no idea. It's just floating out there by Birch Creek, though. It's not in Harbor Hills."

"My mom cut it out of Harbor Hills, but it *did* belong. That little place actually backs to the far side of this community. In fact, the creek runs just along our eastern fence line.

"Why didn't she include it in Harbor Hills?"

"Because of its history. There was some old codger Van Holt who set up a whiskey still in the side of the hill where the creek starts. He had quite the reputation back then, and my mom wasn't interested in any more drama. Any more history." He paused thoughtfully before continuing. "Anyway, our moms always talked about how they'd like for one of you girls to date me. It was *awkward*, back then. Even now, as I tell you, it's a little awkward."

She thought she detected a flush in his cheeks.

Amelia's eyes grew wide. "Are you *serious*?"

He nodded, a smile forming on his mouth. "It was just a little... I don't know. Matchmaking thing, I guess. But your mom never talked about it again after that year. The year Kate got pregnant, I guess. So my mom dropped it, too."

"Was it Kate she wanted you to date?" Amelia asked, her heart sinking.

Michael dipped his chin, "It was the *actress*. That's how she referred to you when we were in school. The little actress."

"How did she even know I was into drama? I mean, I only ever met your mom once or twice out around town. Maybe only once. I didn't know her."

"My mom had her hand in every pot in town. Why do you think the Birch Harbor auditorium is named Van Holt Theater?"

Amelia shrugged. "The mayor?"

"No. Mila Matuszewski. She gave a lot. To the school. The country club. *Me*, of course."

"Including dating advice?" Amelia asked.

He grinned. "Never dating advice. But she was happy to host that party. And if you were going to be there, she didn't mind pretending it was a secret party. She kept it for us. For me."

"Kept what?"

"She let all the partygoers think they were at some weekend party up at my house while my folks were out of town. And she never said anything about that. Or about how much I liked you. She never meddled. Just kept it in her heart. Like a little wish, I suppose." His gaze turned dreamy, and he glanced away. "I think your mom might have had that, too, Amelia. A wish for you." He looked back at her. "It just got lost in the other drama of the time."

Amelia's chest warmed at the touching thought of her own mother having some small interest in Amelia's love life, too, even as a teenager. Amelia didn't have many of those memories. From the age of fourteen on, Amelia's love life seemed irrelevant to Nora Hannigan. All focus went to Clara. And Kate's survival.

Amelia frowned. "But wait a minute. Back up. You *knew* we were in the library. If it was effectively *your* gun, how come you never asked me about it?"

He blew out a sigh. "When I realized it was gone, it was too late. I never used that thing, you know." He gestured to the table. "By the time I went looking for it and couldn't find it, I wasn't positive I'd even left it in the library at all. I certainly didn't suspect that you and your friends had it. I mean when I came in there that night, I had hoped to have a moment alone with you, Amelia."

She swallowed. "So you *did* like me?"

Laughing lightly, he nodded. "Well, yeah. Once my mom planted that seed, it was all I could do to shake it."

"But you dated other girls in high school. And college. And after."

"Of course I did. Back then, all I had was a crush. But think about it: I didn't come in there looking for trouble—or troublemakers. I came in there looking for you. When you shimmied out and left, that was it. I accepted it. Moved on. The gun didn't even enter my mind."

A little disappointed that he hadn't fought for her back then, she gestured to the piece now. "Well, are we even sure *this* is the one? That this is yours? Or Mila's, I mean?"

He reached for it, popped the cylinder out, and held it toward Amelia.

Her eyes finally focused on a faint engraving on the face of the open cylinder.

Mila.

Amelia smiled. A sad smile. A smile for a woman like her mother. Then she asked, "Why not her full initials? Or her last name? There could be other Milas."

Shaking his head, he chuckled. "This was my mom. Trust me. She never really knew her identity. Was she a Van Holt? A Matuszewski? Neither?"

"She was just Mila," Amelia whispered.

Michael smiled.

"That's why you love history so much. You want to learn more about the origins of Birch Harbor? Your mother's roots?"

He shrugged. "I guess so."

"Michael." Amelia splayed her hands on the table, her eyes down. She licked her lips.

"Mhm?"

"What if you had known I'd taken the gun? Back then, I mean? Or... or even now? What if you had known? Would it... would it change things between us?"

"If I had known then that you took it—or even if I had learned later on—I wouldn't have said a thing," he answered. His hand crept across the table toward hers until it rested on top. His fingers curled around Amelia's.

Her eyes flashed up. "Why not?"

"It would have ruined my chances."

"Your chances of what?" She grinned, and her heart raced. There was no question in Amelia's mind that she loved and adored Michael. And maybe, just maybe, he would overlook her stupid past and continue to love her, too.

"It would have ruined my chances of whatever we're moving toward here."

His face fell dark, and Amelia frowned. She didn't know

if he was talking about her dad or the gun or the lighthouse or *what*.

Suddenly, Michael pulled his hand from hers and shot up from the table. "This is *insane*," he murmured, striding away and leaving her there, confused.

He rummaged in a drawer on the inside of the kitchen bar, and Amelia's gaze turned back to the gun. A stupid symbol of all the bad choices she'd made in her life. Her impulsivity. Her inability to say *no* when she ought to say *no* and *yes* when she ought to say *yes*. A perfect representation of how she had many chances in life to make a good decision but instead, couldn't stop for one moment to think. To do the right thing. The good thing. The thing that would make her happy in the end.

"What's insane? What are we 'moving toward here?'" she asked, her heart still pounding in her chest. What was he looking for?

Michael's face froze, his eyes catching on something in the drawer he'd pulled out. He closed it abruptly. He looked up, and a slow smile spread across his face. "I want to talk to you about something important."

CHAPTER 26—MEGAN

K ate had organized an urgent sister meeting at
the Inn for Monday afternoon.

But once Monday was in full motion, each of
the women was too busy for a meeting. They texted a bit over
the course of the week—Amelia revealed that she had cleared
the air with Michael and the gun (but otherwise kept mum).

Kate thought she was making real progress with Vivi
and had some interesting news about a recent guest.

And Clara and Jake were on their way to date number
three. *No signs of slowing down, either*, she'd written in one
particularly adorable message.

And so, despite the busyness of the changing seasons,
Megan felt good. She and Brian agreed they'd made the
right choice to move to Birch Harbor, to stick together, to
start the house project and to continue on with the matchmaking business. All in all, things were looking up for the
Hannigans and the Stevensons alike.

Later that week, once the contractor broke ground on
their new house, Megan and Brian had begun to stitch

together their plans for *Love at the Lake*. Vendors were booked. The event space secured, of course.

Now, she and Brian were at the field, overseeing the construction team as they poured the foundation. The next thing to do was to promote the event and draw up a list of potential and confirmed attendees. This was Megan's favorite part because with the information she'd garnered from applications, she could pair people off ahead of the event. This would allow her to float around and herd the right people together, like a little matchmaking shepherdess.

They were just two applicants down the list, however, when her phone rang.

Megan frowned at the unknown number on the caller ID. Construction played like white noise in the near distance.

She pressed a finger to her opposite ear. "Yes, this is Megan Stevenson."

"Mrs. Stevenson," the pinched voice on the line went on, "This is Mrs. Adamski at Birch Harbor High. We need you to come into the school. There's been an... *incident*.

THERE WAS no panic like a mother-summoned-to-school-to-deal-with-*an-incident* panic.

Brian drove, quiet and calm. Serious, but unwilling to speculate.

As they drove, Megan tapped out a quick message to her sisters, desperate for someone else's reassurance. Their replies of support came at once. Kate reminded her that surely it was no big deal. Amelia responded with a quick memory of the time she got in trouble for pantsing the lead in *Guys and Dolls*.

Clara didn't answer.

Megan sent a second, private message to her.

Principal called. Incident with Sarah... Do you know anything??? Are you still in class? Can you check on her??

They pulled into the visitor parking lot before Megan ever got a response, and as soon as she looked up from her phone, she saw why.

Standing in front of the building was the principal—*and* Clara.

Megan glanced at Brian, who squeezed her hand and murmured some vague reassurance that didn't stick.

"Mrs. Stevenson, Mr. Stevenson," Mrs. Adamski greeted.

Clara pressed her mouth into a line, and her eyes narrowed on Megan.

Once inside, all four adults shuffled into the principal's office. Megan, Brian, and Clara each took a seat in soft-cushioned chairs around the desk. A nameless secretary ushered Sarah in.

Megan tried to communicate wordlessly with her daughter. It sort of worked. Sarah made the face she made when Brian accused her of eating the last cinnamon roll or when a friend called her out for being a bore. A quasi-defensive, wholly innocent expression. Indifferent, even. But now wasn't the time to cop an attitude or act apathetic.

The principal seated herself, laced her fingers on top of her desk, and let out a sigh.

"Mr. and Mrs. Stevenson, the reason we're here is because of an accusation made regarding Sarah." She gestured smoothly across to the dark-haired teenager, slumped in a chair with no seat cushion. An extra metal folding chair. Dug out of the janitor's closet, no doubt.

Perhaps Mrs. Adamski wasn't used to reprimanding big families.

Megan glanced at Clara, whose gaze remained rigidly forward.

"Go ahead," Brian replied, his voice calm but his knee bouncing out of the woman's view.

Out of the corner of her eye, Megan caught Sarah cross her arms over her chest.

"Another student here has indicated a growing concern over Sarah's extracurricular activities."

"Extracurricular activities?" Megan scoffed. "*What* extracurriculars? She helps her aunt some days after school but mostly hangs out at home."

Thoughts of the past weekend—the beach party—came to mind, but Megan buttoned her lips.

"And which aunt would that be?" the woman asked, lowering her chin and peering at Megan over the rim of her glasses.

Did it really matter? Megan wondered.

"My sister Amelia." Her eyes slid to Clara again, who still remained frozen. Her irritation growing, Megan added, "Why is Clara here, anyway? Clara?"

Clara turned her head and frowned at Megan but said nothing.

"Sarah," the principal went on. "Would you care to detail the situation?"

Sarah's arms slid down, and her face crumpled. "It's not *true*," she declared through gritted teeth.

"*What* isn't true?" Megan demanded, now looking at the principal. "I'm sorry, Mrs. Adamski, but can you please cut to the chase? You've got us scared."

"Yes," Brian agreed. "What has Sarah been *accused* of?"

Mrs. Adamski cleared her throat. "There's concern

amongst the student population that your daughter is...
dating an older man."

"Older man?" Brian's voice filled with alarm, and he
leaned onto the desk, his head whipping to Sarah.

Megan's heart plunged into her stomach and
bounced back up into her throat. The conversation she
had with Sarah just a week before crawled back into her
brain. It was *Vivi*. *Vivi* was the one who was into
older men.

Not Sarah.

Certain there was a mistake, Megan looked from her
sister to the principal and then to Sarah. "What does any of
this have to do with *school*?"

At last, Clara's austere posture broke. Her shoulders
sagged forward, and her head turned one degree to Megan.
Megan thought she detected a quick, subtle shake of the
head. But Clara's eyes darted back to her boss, and she
folded in on herself again.

Megan turned her gaze to Mrs. Adamski, frowning at the
woman's inability to form a reply quickly enough. "Is this
'man' a..."

Brian cut in, stealing Megan's thought, "*Teacher*?"

"*No*," Sarah hissed from her corner.

Mrs. Adamski's eyes widened. "Oh, no. No, no. I'm sorry
for alluding to as much." She let out another sigh,
unclasped and re-clasped her hands. "Let me begin again."

Megan and Brian exchanged a look, but Sarah just
shook her head.

"This morning, a student from Miss Hannigan—er,
Clara's first hour asked to come make a report."

Clara finally turned to face Megan full-on, her face
broken, "I had no idea what she was going to say, Megan, I
swear."

"Who was the student?" Megan asked, her eyes moving to Sarah.

"That's irrelevant," Mrs. Adamski returned.

Megan couldn't refrain from huffing, but Brian shot her a severe look.

"What did the student say?" he asked calmly, resting his hand on Megan's knee, although his was the one that continued to bounce.

Mrs. Adamski opened her hands. "The student expressed her concern that one of her classmates was getting 'in over her head'—is the phrase she used—with a gentleman many years Sarah's senior."

"Who is this man?" Brian asked, releasing Megan's knee and leaning closer to the desk, his face stone.

"The reporting student wouldn't say," Mrs. Adamski went on. "But she did suggest he had ties to the school."

"You said it wasn't a teacher," Megan pointed out. With Clara and Sarah entirely mute, she realized she had no option but to dig the truth from the uptight principal—a woman who appeared to demonstrate a minimal degree of common sense... or common courtesy.

"He's not a teacher. But at the time, I didn't have more information than that. I asked the reporting student to clarify, and she simply told me it was the father of another Birch Harbor High student."

"A *father*?" Brian gasped and alarm replaced his solemn affect.

"When the girl wouldn't give me more information, I opened an investigation."

"Which is why I'm here," Clara inserted, running her hands the length of her khaki capris. Megan saw them tremble, and she frowned.

"You know who it is, Clara?"

"Sarah isn't saying anything," Clara answered, lifting her hand uselessly toward the poor teenager.

"And neither is any other student here," Mrs. Adamski added.

"I'm not saying anything," Sarah finally declared, "Because there is *nothing* to say. I'm not *sleeping* with anyone. Or *dating* anyone. Not a teenager *or* a man *or* a dad." Disgust colored her face, and Megan wanted to reach across the office and tug the girl into a tight hug, protect her from the horrors of a false allegation. An indecent one. To hear her own child use that phrase—*sleeping with*—was a moment that Megan would never forget. The crudeness. The undue loss of innocence. Anger rose up inside her.

"And you've given credence to this claim?" Brian asked. Megan could hear his accusation, sense him boiling like she was.

Mrs. Adamski and Clara must have sensed it, too. Clara answered first, "I don't think it has much credit," she admitted, a crook in her eyebrow.

"I just want to ensure that Sarah is *safe*," Mrs. Adamski replied. "If there is no merit to this rumor, then I'll be nothing short of relieved."

"And you figured you'd disregard Sarah's version of this story?" Megan asked, unable to hold back any longer. "And propel her into the spotlight amongst her peers? And teachers, for that matter? You allowed this *lie* to grow."

Brian's hand returned to her knee. "Mrs. Adamski, this is upsetting, as you can imagine. And we tend to trust our daughter. That she makes good decisions, namely, and that she is honest, too. If Sarah says it's false, then should you not consider bringing the other student in here?"

"The troublemaker," Megan added for clarification.

"I will handle this incident from all angles, I assure you, Mr. and Mrs. Stevenson."

"So, Sarah was never in trouble. You just wanted us here to know what students are saying about the new girl?" Megan couldn't squash the bitterness in her words.

Mrs. Adamski held up well to it, though, pressing her hands on the table and reiterating that the only thing she wished to achieve was to ascertain whether Sarah was safe, and if there was anything Megan or Brian would like to do in terms of protection while at school.

"If she's not in danger of some predatory older man, then that's not the protection I'm interested in," Brian answered.

"But what about the fallout?" Megan asked.

"Fallout?" The woman adjusted her glasses and leaned away.

"If there is a student at this school spreading some lie about Sarah dating a classmate's father... I fear Sarah will have bigger repercussions than if the rumor were partly true."

"Megan," Brian hissed.

"Okay, fine," she answered. "Certainly, I hope that the rumor isn't true for Sarah's sake. But I also hope that the rumor spreading is dealt with, too." Her eyes flew to Clara. "Clara? Is this going to be a problem in first period? Should the girls be separated?"

"Now, now, Mrs. Stevenson, we didn't even indicate whether the two girls were in the same class or—"

"I know my daughter's schedule. And I also know who's responsible for this. The whole story is becoming clearer by the minute, Mrs. Adamski, despite your lack of transparency. And, frankly, it gives me great pause in feeling confident about sending Sarah here every morning. Into a veritable lion's den of mean girls. When I went to Birch Harbor—"

Again, Brian cut in. But this time, he didn't water down Megan's fiery reaction. Instead, he added a little fuel, "My wife and I have a sense of what's going on. Surely, it was Viviana Fiorillo who came to make the report?"

Megan turned her attention to her husband, amazed at his perceptiveness. His Adam's apple bobbed, and he glanced at her.

"And Mercy Hennings, too?" Megan added.

"It has nothing to do with Mercy," Clara interjected, her face shattering like glass.

Megan frowned at her sister, concerned by the overreaction playing out on her features. *Was* Mercy involved?

"I disagree," Brian replied, his voice sharp as a knife.

"Brian," Megan warned, her tone low.

At last, the principal visibly fretted. This is what happened when you made a mountain out of a molehill. This is what happened when you trusted an untrustworthy young person. Instead of the innocent new girl.

The principal of Birch Harbor High had effectively incited a family fight. One that Megan refused to lose, because there was no way in *hell* she would let her daughter's senior year turn into some ridiculous small-town scandal.

But Brian turned to Clara instead of the fumbling school administrator. "I want to speak to him."

"To whom?" Mrs. Adamski asked.

"To Jake Hennings."

CHAPTER 27—KATE

Judith Carmichael returned to the Heirloom Inn on Monday to officially make her reservation.

After brief small talk, Kate brought her into the foyer and stepped behind the desk, reviewing her calendar aloud for Judith's benefit.

Still uncomfortable and suspicious, of course, Kate's finger trembled above each open date. There was little use in putting the woman off, and it ended up that Kate's curiosity won out anyway.

Why did Judith Carmichael stop by twice?

Why did she want to stay at the Inn?

Comforted only by the fact that Judith, too, seemed nervous, Kate pointed to a date.

"The first weekend in November?"

"That'll be fine," Judith replied, slipping a hand into her purse. "Do you take a deposit?"

Kate frowned. "Deposit? No, no. Just the reservation will be fine." She paused a beat then measured what she said next. "I trust you."

Judith offered a curt nod in response, but something

flickered across her lips. A recognition, perhaps. Humility, even.

Kate penciled Judith into the guest log and walked her to the door as if everything was perfectly normal.

Matt arrived just as Judith was leaving, but he slipped away from Kate and Judith and into the parlor, his phone pressed to his ear and his face unreadable.

"I'll see you Friday at or after four o'clock, then," Kate said to Judith, as she walked the woman to the front porch.

Judith pressed her lips into a thin smile. "Enjoy your evening, Ms. Hannigan." Then her eyes flitted up the height of the house, and she turned to leave.

Kate realized she forgot something. "Oh, by the way!" she called.

Judith spun on a heel, one eyebrow arched high on her forehead.

"Will it be just you, or will you bring Gene?"

"Just me," Judith answered, her brow falling and her mouth an even line.

At that, Kate didn't know whether to feel better or worse.

"Do you want me to go with you?" she asked Matt.

When she had returned inside, she found him shoving his phone back in his pocket and pacing the parlor.

The school had called. Vivi was in some kind of mix-up. Or trouble. The principal hadn't been clear on the phone. All he knew was that he needed to meet in the front office.

Those kinds of vague invitations were always the worst. The conversations that began with *Can we talk?* The text messages that read *Are you busy?* The phone calls that hung in the air with nothing more ominous than a simple *We need you to come to our office.* Especially if it was the principal's office. Especially when you were the parent.

But Kate wasn't the parent, and this was decidedly *not* her business.

As far as Matt figured, no doubt.

He shook his head and left no sooner than he'd arrived. She grabbed her phone and reopened the text message Megan had sent just a half hour earlier.

Suddenly, her reply that there was nothing to worry about had turned into the biggest untruth of the week. She didn't mean to lie. She just hadn't known what was going on.

She should have, however.

Kate had felt it in her very being that something would come to a head with Vivi. But she thought that something would take shape between them—the would-be stepmother and the edgy teen girl. *Not* others.

Of course, that went out the window if Vivi knew about Clara. If she knew about Clara and Kate and Matt, then what would she do? What would she think? How would she respond?

Could children *snap*?

Of course they could.

Kate tried her hardest to put herself in the girl's shoes. She thought about everything she knew of Viviana Fiorillo.

Vivi was a troubled girl. Her mother left the Island for greener pastures. She was stuck with her dad in a small town. Took the ferry to school as a matter of independence, despite the fact her father had his own boat. Attended St. Mary's, a private Catholic school. Sank her fangs into the sweetest and prettiest girl at the public school—Mercy. Staked her claim to the status of most popular freshman within record time. Tried to take ownership over the new, also pretty, older girl but failed. Learned, at some point, that there was something fishy going on with her father's new girlfriend's family. Had no other family herself.

The most alarming feature of the life of Viviana Fiorillo, however, was how she was highly dependent on very, very few relationships. Just two, in fact.

The one with her father.

The one with her new best friend.

And that was it.

Even the recent reunion between Sarah and the popular clique of Birch Harbor High hadn't redrawn the boundaries. Even if Sarah had spent half the beach party with Vivi, she'd lost her footing in that relationship. Kate was grateful for as much now, for her niece. It was perhaps best they kept a little distance, after all. Depending, of course, on what exactly Vivi had done that warranted a parent visit to the school.

Kate thought hard about what a child like Vivi wanted in her little life. What she needed.

Probably to ensure that she didn't lose either of those two relationships that perhaps felt so delicate to her.

Even though Vivi had a loving dad, three square meals, and extra cash for shopping, a pretty face and a capable mind... she was missing the one thing every young woman needed in life. Someone to call "Mom."

It didn't escape Kate that Clara had no shortage in the Mother Department. Even so, Vivi and Clara (apparently) had hit it off after all. Clara said so herself when she told them all that things had settled in and that Vivi was listening in class, doing her work, and generally contributing to Clara's warm welcome at the high school.

But something else niggled at Kate's brain. Something that didn't sit well with her. Something irrelevant to the Hannigans, it would appear.

Vivi's interest in boys.

Vivi didn't display the usual teenage girl behavior when it came to boys, which was surprising for a girl who had everything she needed to own the boys of Birch Harbor. Absent was that run-of-the-mill squealing about cute passersby or the gushing over a crush. Mercy Hennings had moments of it. Even Sarah had once mentioned some cute local. Not Vivi, though.

It was as if she was saving her energy for something else. Something greater than a high school fling. All her emotion was pent up inside, boiling.

And despite everything Vivi had going for her—her looks, her brain, her good father, and her best friend—her blue eyes sometimes glowed green.

Kate could see it. The jealousy. But she wasn't sure about the focus of it.

Was she jealous that her father had a new woman in his life—Kate?

Possibly.

Jealous that her best friend was on the brink of losing the one thing she shared in common with Vivi?

That's what drew Vivi and Mercy together—neither one had a mother to speak of. If Vivi knew that Mercy's dad was dating, it would change their dynamic. Maybe, in Vivi's mind, it would ruin everything.

Particularly, if Vivi also happened to have a crush on her best friend's father.

At least, Kate thought to herself, Vivi had no idea that Jake Hennings was dating none other than her very own *sister*. Half though she may be.

CHAPTER 28—CLARA

When Brian asked to talk to Jake, Clara nearly lost it. She'd respected her brother-in-law for a very long time, but for him to take things to the next level would mean a fissure in their relationship and in Clara's relationship with Megan.

Anyway, his request had nothing to do with the school. If he wanted to talk to Jake, then he could do that on his own time. Clara prayed that he didn't. And she prayed that none of it was true, but Sarah didn't so much as glance at Clara the whole meeting. Something *was* fishy. There was no doubt of that. Even so, would *Jake* really stoop to that sort of a level?

No way. For starters, he was interested in Clara. And after that, he wasn't some weirdo sleaze. He was a good person. Not the sort who would pick up his daughter's friends. No way. No how. Clara had a gut feeling it was nothing more than a mean-girl rumor, like Megan said. But the problem with Clara was that she hadn't often practiced acting on her gut feeling. Rarely had she trusted it. That was the danger of having lived with Nora for all her childhood and most of her adult life: she'd never been tested. Never taken a real risk. Now, everything felt like a risk. Negating Vivi's report was a professional risk. Trusting it was a personal risk and an affront to her own niece. Not dating Jake risked her ability to ever find another man she held even one ounce of interest in. Dating Jake meant that perhaps she was ignoring the fact that Sarah was a victim and Jake was a two-timer. It was a mess. Plain and simple.

When Megan, Brian, and Sarah left, Clara fell to the brink of tears. But she was a professional and somehow held it together in the lone presence of her boss.

After Mrs. Adamski had ushered the others out, she closed the door and returned to her seat, falling into it and all but breaking character.

Principals were people, too, after all.

"I don't even know what to do next," the woman admitted.

Clara swallowed, then spilled everything she knew. Which was nothing. "With all due respect, Mrs. Adamski, I never once suspected anything. Anything at all. Not regarding Sarah—her behavior has been normal. And not regarding Vivi or her behavior toward Sarah, either. I see these girls out of school, you know. I see Sarah, and I would *know*, you know? If something was wrong, I would *know*.

"Teenagers are the best secret-keepers, Clara," Mrs. Adamski replied. "And if it really is Mercy Hennings' father, wouldn't Vivi know better than you? They are best friends, and Mercy is so meek. It would make sense she'd put Vivi up to telling someone."

Clara shook her head and squeezed her eyes shut. "Mrs. Adamski," she went on, "I *know* Jake Hennings."

"As your student's father, yes but—"

"No," Clara interrupted. "I know him personally, too."

Mrs. Adamski's mouth snapped shut, and her eyes danced up and down Clara as though the young teacher before her had transformed altogether. Then, she frowned. "How? He's not a local. Surely not a family connection, although that would explain access to Sarah—"

"I'm dating him."

FOUR DAYS LATER, and nothing was resolved. Feelings were hurt. Questions were raised. Relationships were skimming along thin ice.

So, of course, Kate texted every last one of the involved parties and demanded they show up to a family intervention. She declared that she refused to brush whatever happened under the rug. They would face it. Head on. Every last one of them, including the non-family members implicated in the events of the week prior.

When Clara found the audacity to inquire about where, exactly, this so-called intervention would be held, Kate replied that the cottage would be the perfect location, please and thank you.

Clara wanted to say no. She wanted to say *Leave me and my house out of it!*

It would be too full of people. And in too close of quarters.

Clara tried to convince Kate to host at the Inn. Or the lighthouse. Or even out in the open at Megan's field.

If they were all getting together as one big, happy family, to hash out everything that had unfolded, they needed a safe place. Kate could see that.

A cozy, quiet place. Free from distractions, and above all: *private*. The Hannigans already had dirty laundry airing out around town. It was time to get things under control, lest ol' Nora roll over in her grave.

The only place that ticked off all the boxes was Clara's cottage by the creek, of course. And when Kate begged that they host the meeting there, Clara feared another thing: she'd have to see Jake. She couldn't ignore his texts any longer. Or her feelings.

And as much as Clara feared that, she prayed for it, too.

On the day in question, she took care to dress in a comfortable, approachable-but-pretty dress—an apricot-colored tunic. She slipped into beige loafers—the perfect early fall shoe. Kept her makeup simple and sweet and her hair loose and wavy about her neck.

She cleaned the cottage and added a chunky knit blanket to the rocking chair for whichever poor sap got stuck in that seat.

And when the doorbell rang fifteen minutes early, she silently hoped it was a wayward Girl Scout, seven months late and loaded down with a surplus of Trefoils.

But it wasn't.

It was Jake.

Behind him, Mercy.

"Hi," he said through a kind smile.

"Hi," Clara replied. Her face and neck were glowing red, she knew. And her heart raced in her chest. To anchor herself, she stared past Jake at his sweet daughter. The one who didn't deserve to be caught up in all the theatrics that the Hannigan family seemed incapable of escaping lately. Clara offered a small wave to Mercy, who remained beside her dad's car.

"She's nervous," Jake said. "I wasn't sure if I should bring her, but she told me she wanted to defend us."

Clara frowned at him. "You two don't need any defense. You didn't do anything wrong."

He dropped his voice. "No, she wants to defend you and me."

In the time since Vivi made her fateful report, Clara and Jake hadn't spoken a word to each other directly. He'd texted her, but she had no clue how to respond. Not after the allegations. Not now.

Neither did Clara see or directly speak with Megan or Sarah, who in some way held her accountable for the indecent events. It was just as well, since Clara had started to wonder if there really may be some truth to the whole thing. Did Sarah *like* Jake? Did she think she had a chance with him? If so, what did that mean? About Sarah and about Clara? And about Jake?

After all, rumors often were hatched from reality, rather than out of thin air. No, Clara didn't suspect Jake of any foul play, but she didn't like to be caught up in bad business. And her sisters and her niece, and her student—they were all just a bubbling batch of bad business, if you asked Clara.

But that was days ago, now, and in the time that had passed, so too had other things. Other changes. Clara only knew as much because of the family group chat and her own inside scoop as a teacher.

Matt Fiorillo kept Vivi home from school, for starters. At least, that was how Kate professed to describe her suspension. Clara knew from the principal what the disciplinary action turned out to be. It wasn't a parental decision. It was a school one.

Jake forbade Mercy from talking to Vivi *or* Sarah.

Megan and Brian rethought everything from *Love at the Lake* to building a house to sending Sarah to Birch Harbor High.

Less dramatically, the Inn was booked through the weekend, and Kate made some vague references to a special guest. Clara didn't care.

Then there was Amelia, who—for once in her life—was the least interesting person in the family, having nothing much to add to the drama except for a few tidbits she hoped to share about the yearbook discovery. No one cared about that, either, though, which all but turned her irrelevant.

And all the while, Clara had navigated the waters of high schoolers, becoming acutely aware of their new teacher's personal life—*dating* life, specifically. Surprisingly, however, the whole thing did wonders for her popularity as a faculty member. That's what happened when a pretty young teacher found herself as fodder in the teenage grapevine. That she had a romantic affair in the works was big news. That it was with one of the students' fathers was bigger. And finally, that one of the senior girls was mixed up in all the action sealed the deal. Suddenly, Miss Hannigan was the most exciting teacher in the history of Birch Harbor High.

Vivi was to return to school on Wednesday, and that was the event that triggered Kate's insistence that they "get together and hash things out."

Clara wasn't a hashing-out type of person. And she really was nervous to see Jake again. Especially now that he had suggested that both she and he needed some form of defense... and that even Mercy knew it and was offering her help, the poor thing.

"Did *we* do something wrong?" Clara asked him.

He shook his head. "I hope not."

She nodded. Clara hadn't done anything wrong. Even if Megan, Brian, and Sarah seemed to think so. Had Jake? Her gut said no. Her family loyalty said yes. And the moment Clara realized that—that it was her family who was inadvertently wedging themselves between her and what might be someone special—she let out a breath. And smiled.

"Is she going to come in?" Clara gestured past Jake to Mercy.

"In a bit," he replied. She wanted us to speak alone. Or, maybe, I guess, she wanted to be alone while you and I spoke. I'm still not sure which."

Clara inhaled and exhaled, worrying her fingers together until she managed to meet Jake's stare. "We have a little while until the others are due. Should we walk and talk?"

Jake agreed, and Clara pushed the door open. "Mercy," she said, lifting her voice across the short distance. "Come in and make yourself at home. We'll be back soon, okay?"

Once Mercy shuffled in, Clara and Jake stepped off the porch and headed past the small clearing, toward the creek.

For some moments, they were quiet. A sigh escaped Clara's mouth every few paces, though, as if she couldn't get her breath.

Soon, they found themselves standing at the edge of the running water.

"Do you come out here often?" Jake asked.

A chilly breeze curled through the trees and whipped a strand of her hair across her mouth. Clara slid a finger between her lips to free it and shook her hair back. She rubbed her hands up her arms. "Not really. I suppose I should."

"It's beautiful," he replied, turning to her. "Oh, you're

cold. Here." He pulled her into his body, less out of affection and more out of service. The gesture had the same effect as if they were on their third date. The break in tension. The physical contact. Clara couldn't tell if it made her colder or hotter, and she regretted everything about the past few days. Ignoring his messages. Holing up in the cottage yet again, like a recluse.

She considered what she might say to turn the tide back now, but nothing appropriate came to mind. Instead, she pointed across the creek to an iron fence line. "See that?"

He nodded, squeezing her again. "Is that the edge of Birch Harbor or something? Are we caged in here?" He laughed lightly, and she did too.

"It's Harbor Hills. That's where the country club is. It's a gated community."

"Oh, right," Jake replied.

"I never even knew how close the cottage was to it," Clara remarked, her body temperature evening out with the mundaneness of their conversation. "My mom went to the country club almost every day. It was, like, her safe haven or something."

"Then how did you not know you were close to it?" he asked.

She nodded, as though she'd been waiting for the chance to explain herself. "I only went once or twice. When she made me go, you know? And we drove out down our drive and onto Maple Wood Boulevard then over to Harbor Ave. and then of course, we cut up Cherry Tree Lane and through the gate and turned right... It was a long way to get to the entrance, and the country club is on the far side of the community. This is just the very back of it. You never would know how close you were, especially if you're like me."

"What do you mean?"

Clara grinned, more at herself than at the question. "I don't go outside much, and I have no sense of direction." Even as she said it, she realized those were two things she wasn't proud of. Things she might like to change about herself.

He squeezed her again, and then his hand slipped down her back as he turned to face her. "Clara," he whispered. She kept her gaze down, but Jake brought his thumb and forefinger to rest beneath her chin, lifting it up. Her pulse stilled at his touch. She didn't realize they were this close to some form of reconciliation. A second chance when they hadn't even seen through their first chance. Jake went on, his voice quiet but firm. "What happened with Vivi and Sarah at the school—that has nothing to do with you and me. You do know that, right?"

She shook her head. "That's not true," she protested, knitting her eyebrows together and looking up at him. "Maybe they didn't name you directly, if that's what you're talking about, but I was there. Sarah is my niece. Those girls are my students. It has *everything* to do with me. I have to go to school now like a teenager rather than a teacher. The kids look at me like I'm Vivi's competition or something. Or the person who tattled on the new girl. My own sisters seem to hate me."

"They don't hate you. It's an awkward situation, that's all. Time will heal it. Today is a good start. We can clear the air, and we can move on."

Her mind shot to her oldest sister. The one in the hardest position of all, no doubt. The one handling it the best she could. "But what about Kate and Matt? How can they move on? And if they can't move on, what will happen? Will everything fall apart?" She shook her head, ashamed to be spilling her guts to this man she still barely knew. Well, perhaps she didn't *barely* know Jake.

After all, he was a good father—Mercy still adored him, despite the scandal. A good teacher—the SCUBA lesson. A good marina manager—his employees loved him.

And she knew other things about Jake, too. Things she had learned over the course of two dates. Two whole occasions spent with the one goal of getting to know each other, in fact. She knew how much his heart hurt after losing his wife. How the only way he could get through the pain was to start fresh. How the water brought him down to earth—which she pointed out as being distinctly ironic. She knew, too, what his hands felt like on the small of her back. How his eyes lingered on her, and how he flushed when she caught him looking.

Clara knew what his lips felt like on hers. How he tasted in the middle of a dive... and in the middle of a walk on the beach.

And she knew she was falling for him. But none of that meant she ought to reveal just how screwed up her family was. And how ashamed she could be.

But somehow, he made it all better.

"Things only fall apart if you let them, Clara," Jake answered, his gaze narrowing on her. "You have more control of your life than you realize. His hand dropped from her chin, and he frowned. "I'm here today not just to help smooth things over for Mercy—for her friendships and her relationship with you, Clara. I'm here to make things work for us, too."

Clara looked down at the creek then back to the cottage, then finally let her gaze fall back on Jake. "What if today goes badly?"

It was a challenge, she knew. And he did, too, because he dropped his hands and took a step back. His face grew dark.

"Clara, do you think I had an affair with your *niece*?"

She waved her hands across her chest frantically. "No, no, no. That's not what I mean at all. At *all*." Her heartrate went into overdrive. She didn't mean it, either. But how could he understand what she *did* mean? The only way for him to understand was to try to explain, but she was losing him.

He'd taken another step back, rubbed his hand across his mouth and turned toward the cottage, assessing his decisions, too. Assessing how he felt about her, no doubt.

She grabbed his arm and neared him. "Jake, what I mean has nothing to do with you. I mean things might go bad with my family."

He frowned.

"I mean that they are... insular. Protective. Megan and Brian are riled about this whole thing, and you could see some ugly behavior in there."

"You think I can't handle a little family feud?" he asked, his voice lighter now.

She shrugged. "I don't know. When I look at you and Mercy, I see this perfect little pair—a happy father and daughter making their way in the world. A quiet life. A good one. And when I step outside myself and look at my family, I see chaos. We're a mess, Jake."

"Your family are good people, Clara. And if Megan and Brian weren't upset about the whole thing, I'd be more worried. I'm a father, first, you know." His expression took on another shadow, but he shook his head. "Look, Clara, I mean what I said. I'm here for Mercy. And I'm here for you and me. And if you can't accept that, then I can't do anything about it."

Clara squeezed her eyes shut momentarily, inhaled deeply, then stepped closer to him. As she slowly let out the breath and opened her eyes, she saw him searching her for some answer.

But she couldn't speak it. So instead, she ran her hands up his arms, over his shoulders, wrapped them behind his neck and pulled herself up.

And then she stopped breathing. And she kissed him.

CHAPTER 29—MEGAN

After the meeting in the principal's office, Megan talked Brian out of calling Jake Hennings. But it didn't take much since Sarah swore up and down that positively, absolutely *nothing* about Vivi's claim was true.

Not only had Sarah had zero interaction with Jake, but if what she said was accurate, then Jake also wasn't a fan of his daughter's best friend. Sarah even said that Vivi admitted she wasn't invited to their house. Mercy went as far as to suggest that her dad downright discouraged her from having much to do with Vivi. He preferred that Mercy be a quiet, individualistic girl, even.

With that assurance, Brian and Megan tried to let it go. But it was hard. Having such a seed planted could do damage to a parent's brain. They started to see Sarah through a new lens. An adult one. And even if she was on the precipice of turning eighteen, she was very much their little girl. What was harder, however, than erasing the image of Sarah cavorting with a grown man, was the image of her navigating shark-infested waters in school, dodging whispers and ducking beneath cruel rumors.

All this, according to Sarah, was partly why she was in and then out with the younger group. Sure, she didn't care to hang out with freshmen. But even more than that, Sarah's addition added a kink to the dynamic, highlighting the fact that Vivi wasn't a welcome piece of Mercy's world. Why Mercy continued to befriend Vivi was no wonder: they each contributed something to the other.

Mercy needed Vivi to survive high school high society. Vivi needed Mercy so she had a partner in crime—someone to leverage her onto the cheerleading squad. After all, loners didn't become cheerleaders. Someone to label as a best friend. And someone with an especially popular and attractive father to swoon after and pin her hopes and dreams on.

And mainly, someone who, like Vivi, didn't have a mother around.

And that's why Megan agreed to a family meeting. To wade through the drama and ensure that when Sarah returned to school on Monday, she would be safe. Because if she weren't, Megan didn't know what she would do. Especially since there wasn't exactly a second high school in the vicinity.

THEY ARRIVED PRECISELY ON TIME. Not early so as to make poor Clara even more of a nervous wreck than she already was. Not late to peeve Kate.

Brian had to all but drag Sarah inside, and that's when Megan wondered if this was a terrible idea. Should the grownups subject the girls to each other? Would they actually be successful in clearing the air? Was Kate's plan a bad one? Could teenage girls be made to make up?

But once they stepped into Clara's cottage, the atmosphere set Megan at ease immediately.

It was like a family get-together rather than a come-to-Jesus. Clara had baked cookies and was busy setting a platterful on her coffee table, next to a prettily fanned-out stack of paper napkins. Kate was pouring glasses of iced tea from the kitchen bar.

Two candles glowed from the center of the kitchen table, emanating notes of apple cinnamon and reminding Megan that fall was upon them. An assortment of fresh-cut fruit and veggies and cheese and crackers framed the candles. Back on the kitchen bar was a seasonal medley of pumpkins, squash, and gourds, and in front of them sat two apple pies.

It might be overmuch for a Sunday gathering, but the weather was changing, and big questions still hung in the air. Megan withdrew a bottle of wine from her grocery sack and set it on the kitchen table.

In the corner of the living room, Michael and Jake stood chatting, and if Megan didn't know any better, she'd have thought there was a ball game on TV and it was half-time and everything was good and normal, and Sarah was still an innocent girl with friends, and Clara was still dating a kindly single dad, and Kate's boyfriend's daughter was nothing more than a pretty teenager with a chip on her shoulder.

Megan couldn't decide if the contrast was a good thing or a bad thing—the cold conversation that would be staged in such a warm and cozy setting. To drag Sarah back through her own small drama felt like bad parenting, but Kate had assured her that the girls were old enough to join in the conversation about what happened. They were at the center of it, after all. And to Kate's credit (and Clara's, it would appear), they tried to make the ambience such that people were passing a bowl of chips rather than a box of tissues.

As Brian and Sarah joined her at the table, their attention easily and immediately shifting to the food, Megan reminded herself that if nothing else, they were among family. And that was more than she could have said back in the suburbs a year prior.

"The Stevensons are here!" Kate trilled merrily from the kitchen, steering two glasses of tea in their direction. "Welcome, welcome! Sit, sit! Or grab some food. Whatever you prefer. This is all very casual." She dipped her chin to Megan once Brian and Sarah accepted their drinks. "Come on, Meg, come get your tea."

Megan followed her sister and whispered, "Where's Vivi and Matt?"

Once in the kitchen, Kate stirred a second pitcher of tea. "They'll be here."

Megan let out a breath she didn't realize she'd been holding. "They're late."

"I know, Megan. Don't worry. I talked to Matt. They're coming."

"Kate, this is incredibly awkward. Are you sure it's a good idea?" Megan hissed, waffling back and forth between comfort and discomfort—anticipation and dread. She lifted her gaze to the others, who carried on as usual. Sarah and Mercy had found each other and seemed to be chatting, even though they sat on opposite sides of the couch. Megan had been under the impression that Mercy was forbidden from having anything to do with Sarah. Had things softened there? Was there a light at the end of this emotionally exhausting tunnel of teenage drama and flying accusations?

She watched Brian skirt around the kitchen table, adding bits of food to his plate. Would he sidle up to Jake? Or would all the calm turn to craziness and the two wind up in some childish fist fight on the front porch?

Kate dropped the ladle onto a dishtowel, ran her hands on a second one, then turned to face Megan. "Yes. This *is* a good idea. We aren't doing the Nora thing, Megan."

"What do you mean?"

"Mom was notorious for sweeping her problems under the rug. Writing them down in a diary and scattering the pages in secret spots throughout her properties like a gossip fairy sent from the past. I refuse to do that to the girls."

"Do what?" Megan asked.

Kate sighed. "To pretend everything is okay today to preserve some fantasy about the future that may or may not exist. Megan," Kate went on, "we can either ignore what Vivi did, or we can ask her why she did it? We can come together. Eat, drink, and share in each other's lives in a way that means something for once. Do you ever remember Mom doing that? Dragging us together after an argument? Making us sit together in a circle so we could fight and laugh and cry and just *talk*?"

Megan blinked, then shook her head. "No."

"Well, that's what we're going to do. Okay? And if we want to grow our relationships rather than hamstring them, then you've got to give Vivi a chance."

"She's awful, Kate," Megan answered, her defensiveness of Sarah growing by the minute. Sure, Megan could go along with a little family venting session. But to allow in this cruel outsider? This girl who was hellbent on undermining not only her daughter's social success, but also her younger sister's career? "And what about Clara? How does Clara feel about this?"

At that, Clara materialized behind them, as if by magic. "I'm a little scared, I'll admit."

Megan opened to her, taking in the youngest of the Hannigan four. She wore an orange-ish dress, and her cheeks were flushed. Her hair hung loose and pretty, and she seemed... *not* scared. "You look gorgeous," Megan replied.

Clara grinned. "Thank you."

Megan let a smile curl up her cheeks. She could see plain as day why Clara wasn't hiding in the back bedroom. The look of love washed over Clara's face, and it was quite obvious that whatever had happened regarding Vivi's accusations against Jake... it was water under the bridge. That much was obvious. And if she was fearful about something, it sure as heck wasn't keeping her from shining that day.

"I think we're all a little scared, but here's the thing," Kate paused and took a breath. "This is bigger than the rumor Vivi started."

Megan and Clara looked at Kate in tandem. "What do you mean?"

"If Vivi were just some stranger's daughter, then we could write her off. We could count her as a mean girl and go on our merry way. But she's not some stranger's daughter." Kate's voice broke into a tremble. "She's the daughter of the love of my life."

Megan's face softened. Her shoulders relaxed. Maybe that secondary goal would help her hang in there. Maybe it would relieve some pressure to know that it wasn't only Sarah against Vivi or Vivi against Clara. It was the Hannigan family *for* each other. Even Kate, who was a veritable third party in the current drama.

Megan saw it clearly. This was Kate's chance to save the one thing that continually slipped through her fingers.

Matt Fiorillo.

"I get it," Megan said, fortified. "I totally get it. You and Matt. We have to fix this for you, too."

"But," Clara interjected, her confidence bending a little, a break in the fresh façade, "what if we can't change Vivi? What if Matt can't fix her?"

Megan looked at Clara, impressed by her articulation of the one fear that any woman had in life: the fear that people were who they were. That you couldn't help them be better. You couldn't mold them into the thing you needed them to be.

But Kate narrowed her gaze defensively. "What are you saying, Clara? Vivi is not *evil*."

Clara didn't back down. "Kate, I have to see these girls day in and day out at my job. I have to face them. And Vivi has all but become my own personal bully, even when she's not there. After the whole thing, my colleagues see me differently. I'm no longer a teacher. And while that's not a bad thing in terms of my popularity among students, I've practically become one of them! And that's *not* good. Obviously." Clara was heated, but she regained control, lowering her voice and flicking a glance from Megan to Kate. "And that's not all, Kate. Don't you see what she did? She tried to make sure Jake and I don't date. It's the same problem you're having. Vivi wedges herself between couples. Like a snake. Can you really change that in a child?"

Kate crossed her arms over her chest and cocked her head to one side and, in her body language, Megan saw their mother. The hard, cold posturing that Nora Hannigan would put on when challenged or confronted. The affect that could freeze hell. The one that helped turn her daughters into strong young women. "I would think *you* of all people would believe that children can change. That they can learn. Right?" Kate replied, her voice even and cool.

Clara took in a deep breath and scanned the room. "I do believe children can learn, of course. But... listen. With Jake, well, I've found someone to like. Maybe to love, and if Vivi ruins that then—"

"Then you didn't have much to begin with," Megan said.

CHAPTER 30—AMELIA

Amelia had been dubbed the official mediator, partly because she wasn't shy and partly because she had the least to lose.

Now, however, she felt like she had the most to lose. With the conversation she and Michael had had just a week before and the new information coming up on Judith Carmichael—she was *on to* something in her life.

But she was also on the brink of undermining her own progress by letting Michael in to see just how dysfunctional her family was. She shouldn't have invited him.

Then again, Michael and Amelia had something to share with the group, too. And there may not be another family get-together in the near future. Not with how busy everyone was.

So, she bit the bullet and told him to come. After all, she recalled her mother doing something similar. For every family Christmas dinner or Easter Brunch, Nora Hannigan had a little secret. A little plan.

She would bring a new person to the bunch—a third

party, of sorts. Someone to keep everyone on their best behavior. Someone to perform for. A new neighbor or a friend from the country club. Never a date, per se, but always a person the girls had never met and who didn't necessarily fit in their lives. There was hope that this new person would become Nora's best friend. Or that the kindly gentleman would court Nora after seeing just how perfectly behaved her daughters were. How perfect the whole family was.

And then they'd never see the guest again. A blip on the radar.

Michael wasn't a blip on the radar. He was part of Amelia's life, and if she had anything to say about it—which she did, it turned out—then he was there to stay.

So, for now, he tucked himself onto a kitchen chair behind the sofa, a distant but familiar presence. Available to help, not to watch and judge.

"I know you'll all think this is goofy." Amelia started from her seat on the rocking chair. It was an uncomfortable seat, but she didn't need to be comfortable. She needed to be on edge to handle things. She looked around the room, her gaze landing on Clara and Kate—who sat together on the piano bench—situated in front of the television to form a nearly perfect circle. Beyond them in the armchair was Vivi, emotionally isolated. Next to her in a kitchen chair sat Matt, then on the sofa were Brian, Sarah, and Megan. And nearest Amelia, propped rigidly in two more kitchen chairs were Jake and Mercy. It wasn't a dynamic arrangement, but it *was* an intentional one, positioning each of the three girls separately and allowing for the adults to exit stage left when the time came.

Amelia went on. "Today, we aren't going to take turns talking or write a secret note to someone in the group to share a feeling or an apology or whatever. We're going to... well, we're going to be *normal* for once."

The others turned serious expressions on her, but no one spoke.

"That's right. This isn't an intervention. It's a gathering. A chance to bond. I mean, I know this is awkward, but the reason I sat everyone down here—the 'intervention' part of this, I mean—is to give the girls a little history lesson, all right?" She looked at Michael, who nodded from his seat in the back.

"I like that." It was Mercy who spoke, surprising them all.

Slowly, Amelia nodded, a smile pricking her lips. "Right, yes. It'll be nice. Clara baked cookies, and Kate set out a bunch of snacks on the table. We've got iced tea and some apple cider, and if you need to get up at any point, please do. Quietly, of course. But I was assigned to be the leader, and that's my angle."

Brian held his hand up like a child in class. "A history lesson, Amelia? Are you qualified to give us a history lesson?" His joke broke the surface tension, and a few giggles fell after it.

Amelia smiled. "Not when it comes to real history, no. But when it comes to my family's history of craziness, no one is better qualified."

Again, laughter came and shot ripples through the circle. Adults eased back in their seats. The girls flicked glances nervously at each other, then looked eagerly at Amelia.

After her miniature introduction, a few reached for cookies, and Matt went to grab a drink. Kate and Clara relaxed next to Amelia, who stretched her mouth in preparation for the mini lecture she had to begin.

And then, once everyone had re-settled in, she started.

"This story begins with another drama, one that didn't end as well as this most recent affair." She lifted one eyebrow.

Megan *oohed* from the sofa, winking at Amelia.

"Once upon a time, there was a woman named Nora Hannigan," Amelia continued, her attention flitting from Vivi to Sarah to Mercy, and then to Clara, who didn't know everything she was about to reveal. "Nora was born into a hardworking local family who just so happened to have waterfront property on Lake Huron. This was no stroke of luck, mind you. Nora's ancestors weren't powerful, but they were unrelenting, you see. Way back then, when Birch Harbor was nothing more than a settlement camp along the banks of the lake, a set of families wheeled in and decided it would make for a great home. The Banks. The Van Holts. The Actons. And the Hannigans. After a long, drawn-out fight for the only buildable land on the water, three families came out ahead. The Van Holts, the Actons, and the Hannigans. The Banks, after some sort of brawl and then a near-drowning, were pushed out to the little landmass we now call Heirloom Island."

Vivi yawned across the living room, and Amelia shuffled ahead in the story, always good at reading audiences.

"Many years later, young Nora was born, and her warm and loving parents raised her up to be a good girl. But you see, in the Hannigan family, being a good girl meant giving everything you had to the family. Blind loyalty and hours of work. Her parents enlisted Nora and her siblings to help fix up the house there on the harbor, as everyone knows. Nora herself even buttoned up new drywall and hauled in shiny modern porcelain toilets."

Sarah made a face.

"That's right, before your grandma was the glitzy glam woman you knew, she was just a girl trying to help her family." Amelia winked at Sarah. "But then, when Nora was in high school, things changed. Nora rebelled."

At this transition, Vivi sat up straighter. Amelia watched Mercy frown. Sarah squirmed.

Clara's face turned white as a sheet.

But it had to be said. The whole thing. They had to get out from under the secret once and for all.

CHAPTER 31—SARAH

Sarah knew exactly where Aunt Amelia was taking the story, and she didn't like it. Besides, Vivi already knew the truth about Kate and Clara. Would Amelia go that far? And if she did, how would Vivi react to being confronted with what she'd already learned accidentally?

Aunt Amelia went on, "Nora met a weekender when she was young. Too young. He fell in love with her, I suppose, and that one-sided affection turned into something much more."

Out of the corner of her eye, Sarah saw Mercy wince. Even Sarah knew the girl was a little too young to be wholly comfortable with the concept of pregnancy. Or too old, as the case may be. The matter of a pregnant woman split across age groups, in Sarah's observations. Young girls were thrilled over the idea of a big-bellied mama. Young *women* were wary of it. But the tweeners—girls of Mercy and Vivi's age—shuddered at the thought. To a freshman in high school, a pregnancy meant... well...

"What happened?" It was Vivi who asked, and Sarah noticed just how rapt she was. Taken, it seemed, with Aunt

Amelia and the story. This surprised Sarah, who had only seen in Vivi someone with limited attention span for others and unending focus on herself.

Aunt Amelia clasped her hands in her lap. "Our mother, Nora, got pregnant when she was just your age."

Sarah watched as Vivi's eyes grew even wider with interest. She looked over at Mercy, who also sat in semi-shock.

"Nora's parents wouldn't let her keep the baby."

"Where is the baby now?" Mercy asked, her voice all but shaking.

Aunt Amelia's response was flat and cool, and Sarah felt more at ease with the whole thing. Perhaps she had an advantage, having heard the story first from her parents.

"She lives in Indiana. We don't know her, but she gave me the lighthouse. She's a good person."

"Who's the dad?" Vivi asked, predictably.

"Not Grandpa Wendell, you see. Liesel—that was the baby's name—mistakenly thought Wendell was the dad. That's how she came to own the lighthouse. But she was wrong."

Sarah chimed in, excitement filling her words. "The dad was the old high school principal." She liked being in the loop. It set her above. And to her, the scandal with Grandma Nora felt several degrees removed. Irrelevant, even. She could be excited about it. It didn't change the world for her. Not like it changed the world for her mother and aunts.

"Who is the old high school principal?" Mercy asked. "Does he still live in town?" The conversation was becoming theirs now. Matt had gone to the kitchen to get another drink. Sarah's dad went back there, too. Suddenly, the so-called intervention was breaking up, and it started to feel like story time. All they were missing was a crackling campfire and gooey s'mores. Sarah's stomach grumbled.

"You probably don't know him," Aunt Amelia replied. "His name is Gene Carmichael, and he didn't leave Nora alone for a long time."

"I've had that happen," Vivi interjected.

Sarah scoffed. "You've had a stalker?"

The other girl shrugged. "Maybe you'll have one, too, one day."

Rolling her eyes, Sarah wondered if she would ever come to like Vivi. If Vivi would ever apologize. If there would ever be room for both of them at the high school. Or even in Birch Harbor.

"You see," Aunt Amelia went on. "He became her shadow. But after the adoption, Nora did find her true love. Our dad. Wendell."

"But he left, right? That's what my dad told me." Vivi argued. "How could he be her true love?"

Aunt Amelia shook her head. "We don't know what happened to him. All we know is that he's gone, Vivi. Not that he *left*. It's more complicated than that. When a parent leaves his or her children, it's not an easy choice. And that's assuming the parent chooses to leave at all." Amelia paused and narrowed her stare on Vivi. "I bet you can understand that, right?" She cocked her head, and Sarah immediately recognized the body language.

This was her aunt playing mean girl back at Vivi. Not overtly. Not in a way that made Aunt Amelia cruel or awful. But just enough that maybe... just maybe... Vivi would get the hint. Maybe this would go better than Sarah had imagined it could. She stifled a grin and stole another look at Vivi.

Shrinking back, Vivi frowned and crossed her arms, but she didn't answer.

Which meant that she absolutely did understand what

Aunt Amelia was saying. She did understand that she wasn't alone in her own history of personal scandals and problematic parents.

Could Vivi be more than her past, too? Was there more to her than a rumor-starting brat who all but wrecked Sarah's life?

Sarah still wasn't sure. But now, as she listened to what her aunt was trying to say, Sarah didn't quite feel angry at Vivi anymore. She felt angry about what happened. But Sarah still had both parents—together. She almost didn't, however. So, instead of anger, sadness colored her opinion of the poor, beautiful island girl who sat gripping the overstuffed arms of Grandma Nora's chair.

"Do you know, Vivi, that our dad went missing during a time in our life that was very complicated?"

Sarah's gaze flew to Clara, who clutched Aunt Kate's hand on the piano bench and whose eyes were turning watery.

When Sarah looked back across the room, she realized that all the men were gone. Jake, Matt, Michael, and her dad. They'd disappeared. Not like Grandpa Acton, but they were gone.

Now, it was just the women left to sort things out.

Maybe this was the Hannigan way.

CHAPTER 32—CLARA

Vivi nodded in response to Amelia's question, and Clara frowned.

She couldn't hold back. "What do you mean you know? What do you know, Vivi?"

All eyes turned on the white-blonde child, who pressed her mouth into a thin line and furrowed her brow. After a moment, she dropped her chin to her chest. "I know Clara is my half-sister. I overheard Kate talking about it after the Fireflies thing."

It was a whisper. A murmur. Barely audible. But it confirmed exactly what Clara had begun to fear.

She wanted to claw Matt Fiorillo back here to answer for all this. It was his problem as much as it was hers or Kate's. And Vivi was his daughter. He should be the one to spearhead the conversation.

But Kate stole Clara's thoughts. "This is my fault," she declared, her voice breaking.

Amelia shifted in the rocking chair, and its creaking broke the tension somewhat. "What is your fault, Kate?"

"I told Matt to keep it a secret. I just... I didn't know how

Vivi would take it. I didn't know when the time would be right. I didn't want it to... to *ruin* things."

"Will it, Vivi?" Amelia directed the question across the room. Clara studied the girl carefully. After so many years of teaching, she thought she could read teenage girls well. Lately, though, she wasn't too certain.

Vivi lifted her chin, and all the vim and vigor and edge about her seemed to rise up and provide her with the gumption she needed to answer such a question as that.

And for a fourteen-year-old who had effectively lost her own mom and grappled with fitting in—despite her beauty and her popularity and her intelligence—she had something else deep inside.

"Maybe," Vivi squeaked, her voice trembling and her eyes wet, "it will fix things."

Clara broke into tears but managed a smile toward Vivi, who was also crying now and—impressively—accepting a hug from Sarah. Sweet Sarah who was brooding and independent and the product of good and loving parents. Her compassion and maturity shone, and Clara realized that the truth wasn't something to fear at all.

The truth, in fact, was something Clara needed.

The truth was that even with the love and support of her three older sisters, Clara was going it alone. Siblingless. And technically motherless.

Maybe she and Vivi had more in common than they even knew. Maybe, instead of being alone in their pain, they could manage it together. With Matt—who returned to the circle, tearful and short of breath as he tugged his daughter into a hug. And then, when Clara stood from her piano bench—the bench she shared with the only mother she had left—Matt crossed to her. And hugged his other daughter, too.

CHAPTER 33—KATE

Amelia had dropped the ball.

She claimed to be more improvisational than organized, which was largely true, but Kate should have stepped in right after the intervention—after everyone kissed and made up, and things were looking good again.

Amelia had done nothing in the way of making arrangements for a grand opening, Kate quickly learned. And with Megan too focused on her own event, there had been two choices: cancel the grand opening or do as originally planned and merge it with *Love at the Lake*.

Kate discovered all this when Megan came to her with a big, fat problem: very few clients or guests had RSVP'd for the matchmaking event.

The only logical thing was to do what the Hannigan women did best: make it a family affair.

So *Love at the Lake* would move forward just as *Fireflies in the Field* had. All hands on deck.

In the meantime, other parts of the Hannigans' lives were settling in.

The girls were preparing for Homecoming, which worked out well enough. Their return to school was largely uneventful, overshadowed by the next big scandal at Birch Harbor High: a group of senior boys broke into the marina overnight and took a speed boat out for a joyride, making waves with the community and with the administration.

Clara was relieved to be free of the spotlight, as was Jake. She revealed to her sisters that they had decided to make their third date for the weekend of Megan's event. This worked out in everyone's favor, because they could set the tone for a date night vibe but also come back into the fold as a couple, free from the events of the preceding weeks and on the brink of setting sail into the sunset together. Hopefully.

So, there they were—Kate, Amelia, Megan, and their menfolk—at the lighthouse, setting up for *Love at the Lake*. Amelia twittered about half-uselessly, caught up in rehearsing her opening spiel and checking frantically on their exhibits.

Yes, Amelia and Michael did manage to pull that off—historical exhibits. Even though it was an outdoor event, with the nip in the air, they had decided to stick to the lighthouse itself, hanging photographs and balancing informative plaques in the generous space on the ground floor.

Amelia planned to station herself at the door there and act as a docent. Michael promised he'd hang around the area to help with any questions. They would be sort of relegated to the lighthouse together, which was okay with Kate, who promised to act as something of a matriarch for the greater event—seeing to it that love-seeking guests would also visit the would-be museum. Even if it was less of a grand opening, Kate saw that Amelia had something there. And in the end, it worked out that she played off the heels of Megan's event. They were better together, it turned out.

Among the modest collection that Amelia and Michael had managed to curate were surprisingly good bits of history. Storied photographs depicting early settlers. Newspaper clippings and portraits. Some artifacts that Michael had uncovered from his mother's collection, including a little wooden desk that could have come straight from a one-room schoolhouse. All charm and no mystery.

Although, when it came to Wendell's case, many unanswered questions persisted.

Initially, Amelia was convinced that Judith Carmichael was the key to it all. Her enrollment at St. Mary's alongside Nora seemed too coincidental. Too sinister.

But Kate new better.

Especially now that Judith had coined herself a "friend of the family," as she had declared in a cryptic announcement at a recent town council meeting.

It wasn't a total lie. Judith had ended her visit to the Inn with a generous proposition. She had asked Kate that a small monument to the Banks family be erected on the beach behind the house—Judith's life goal was to memorialize her family and their undocumented efforts in settling the area.

However, during her visit to the Inn, Kate had detected an undercurrent. There was more there than just a trip down memory lane. Kate could feel it. She could feel it with the iciness. The cool conversation—hovering just above comfort level. She could feel it when Judith had started into her baloney about wanting to support local businesses. Of course, Kate threw that back in her face by reminding Judith of her condemnation of Megan's business.

That's when Judith had launched into the bit about a family memorial and struggling with long-held bitterness and hard feelings and that she was *trying* to do right by the town and her own ancestors and that she hoped to hold all others accountable to a high standard, as well.

Yada, yada.

Naturally, Kate didn't buy it. So, she balked about a Banks family tribute.

And that's when Judith made an offer: she'd help with Amelia's museum. She had insider information on the history of the town and the Island. Artifacts of her own to contribute. She'd love to act as the unofficial—or official—Island expert for Birch Harbor Lighthouse and Museum. She'd open an account and help manage donations. She'd work hard for Amelia. Or rather, *with* Amelia. Judith's words.

When Kate offhandedly mentioned it to her sisters, Amelia didn't hesitate to jump on the opportunity. After all, to Amelia, Judith was more than a kindly donor. She was suspect number one in the Case of the Missing Father.

But Kate had made Amelia promise that, at least for this event, she'd keep quiet.

And so there they were, Kate hovering about the buffet table and drink station. Megan had opted for a fall theme. Alongside the usual veggie trays and cheese and crackers, they offered spiced cider, hot cocoa, warm apple pie, and a s'mores station near the bonfire the men had raging at the lip of the lake.

After organizing a rustic aluminum canister with roasting sticks, she checked in with the DJ and tested the heat lamps. Meanwhile, Amelia and Michael tended to the lighthouse, and Megan and Brian stood at the guest check-in, reviewing the list of attendees.

Half of the list was comprised of contacts and relations, but that was just as well. Brian had made good progress on their app, *Fireflies*, and they expected to have some people show up just before the party started—or even during it. It depended on when app users logged in with their GPS. That was the idea of the app, after all. To pin yourself to a locale and see who in the area was also looking for love. On location or in their own backyard.

It turned out, once the night was underway, quite a few people were. An hour into the night, the beach was packed. Strangers galore and some familiar faces, too.

Kate hadn't spotted Clara and Jake yet—but they were supposed to be there with bells on, as Clara had promised.

CHAPTER 34—CLARA

Clara had volunteered to see the girls off to the Homecoming dance, and she took great pleasure in it. With Kate and Megan setting up for the lighthouse event, Clara got to be the one to add finishing touches to hair and makeup before Sarah's, Vivi's, and Mercy's dates arrived to collect them and sweep them off to the high school gym.

Balance had taken the place of chaos, and Clara could see that Sarah was thriving in her role as leader for the younger two. With Jake's blessing, Mercy was back in the fold, and things were good. Even with Vivi in the mix.

Jake arrived with Mercy and Vivi and their dresses in tow, and Sarah drove herself up to the cottage. Before he left, Clara asked Jake to help her lug the hope chest upstairs. Without her hovering sisters, she had free rein to rummage through it. And who knew what might be inside? Hopefully, Clara declared to the girls as they busied themselves with fake eyelashes and hot irons, the balance of Nora's costume jewelry lurked within.

Leaving the chest in Nora's room per Clara's instructions,

Jake pecked her on the cheek, bid farewell to Mercy and the other two, and slipped out the front door after promising to return for Clara in a little while, once the "coast was clear." Clara chuckled, shooed him down the porch steps, and returned to the girls.

"Pearls," Vivi said to Sarah as they squeezed together in front of the standing mirror in Nora's room. "They're so retro, and your dress is vintage, right?"

Sarah gave Clara a look. "Did Grandma leave behind pearls?"

"I don't know about pearls, but we can find something dated, I'm sure." Clara laughed to herself and cracked open the heavy lid, dropping to the floor and pawing through Nora's hope chest.

But as soon as she started searching, she froze.

Hidden underneath a ziplocked bag of doilies, there sat a time-worn composition book.

Scrawled across the cover in Nora's classic script: *Wendell Acton, 1992.*

"Did you find anything?" Sarah asked, peering over her shoulder into the musty chamber. The one that had held the yearbook. The one that couldn't possibly have even *more* secrets buried away.

Clara let the heavy wooden lid fall shut and swiveled. "No," she snapped. Then she pressed her hand to her head. "Sorry, no. But you know what?"

Sarah frowned.

"I think I have something even better in my vanity." Clara shooed her niece into her bedroom and rummaged through her own stash, finding diamond studs instead.

She could hardly focus for the next half hour. Nodding and smiling wordlessly as the girls giggled and gossiped, fretted over limp locks and uneven eyebrows.

Once pictures were over and the girls left, whispering among themselves and enthralled to have their own night out—complete with its eventual little dramas and romantic interludes—Clara collapsed on the sofa.

The image of the notebook clung to her brain traumatically.

She could give up her own night, dive into it. She could reinstate chaos in her family's lives and tip the balance yet again.

Or she could get ready for her date.

It felt like the same position she had been in with the yearbook, and it made Clara wonder if she was the wrong person to own the cottage by the creek.

Or maybe, examined another way, she was the right person.

Because Clara Hannigan refused to let the past get in the way of the present.

Not ten minutes later, a knock came at the door.

Her present.

CHAPTER 35—MEGAN

With the event well underway and enough guests to mingle independently of her, Brian and Megan helped themselves to pie and cider, settling at a table near the lighthouse.

Within minutes, they were joined by Amelia and Michael, Kate and Matt, and then Clara and Jake—the new couple, fresh and giddy and uncomfortable in a good way.

Megan felt proud to see all of them happily paired off, but something was in the air. Something besides sparks from the fire. A hint of trepidation. A shade of fear, even. She couldn't pin it down.

"So, Amelia," Megan asked after a long sip. "how's the museum? Lots of action?"

Michael and Amelia exchanged a look before he answered for them. "Well, we already caught a set of your clients making out on the observation deck."

"That's... good for me," Megan acknowledged before she and Kate fell into a fit of laughter. Even Clara grinned from ear to ear.

"But not for me," Amelia complained. "I don't want this place to become Lookout Point."

"What's Lookout Point?" Clara asked.

"Where we used to go make out on the south shore near St. Patrick's Catholic," Kate answered, laughing and snuggling up against Matt. Megan grinned at the memory. She had heard about it as a girl and visited as a teen—a few times, even. Nostalgia washed over her.

Lookout Point was the sort of place where a couple from the 1950s might drive for a romantic thrill only to leave with a hook attached to the car door handle. The setting combined three disparate atmospheres all at once. It was a teenage escape. A sacred Sunday retreat. And the craggy beach that ran south from it was the most isolated length of shoreline along the western side of Lake Huron.

Sure, countless Birch Harbor lovebirds had made their vows at St. Patrick's. But it was also where you went on the other bookend of life. Funerals were more frequent than weddings, Megan was pretty sure.

The entire slice of Birch Harbor seemed to teeter on the edge of the earth, about to fall into the lake and sink down to the bottom.

The south shore encompassed beginnings and ends and yet nothing much in between. Unless you were a devout parishioner like Nora had been. Megan wondered if she ought to get them registered there. Maybe there was something more to Lookout Point and St. Patrick's than love and death. Maybe there was something to be said for the faith-filled pews of Megan's youth. Those Masses she shared with her sisters before Clara came along. Kate shushing them. Amelia refusing to give her dollar to the collection basket until Nora jerked it from her hand, faked a broad smile, and passed the basket on down the row, past Wendell and to the next Catholic.

As Megan thought about those days, it occurred to her that Amelia's inability to manage or handle her finances and figure out when to spend and when to save and when to give... it started long ago.

"How are The Bungalows?" Megan asked Amelia suddenly. She knew how they were, of course. She lived there. But one of the other tenants had moved out, and it was all hands on deck looking for a replacement. It was Amelia's main source of income, especially now that they saw her museum project would be just that—a museum. Not a business. Not like Megan's. "Has anyone got a lead on a new renter?"

Amelia shrugged. "I've been preoccupied. With this and the Wendell stuff."

Clara cleared her throat. "No news there, right?"

Amelia shook her head. "Nope."

Michael added, "We're not done, though. I'm going to head out to St. Mary's next week and do a little digging on the Judith Carmichael coincidence."

"I'll be interested to hear what you find. I mean, just because they went to St. Mary's together, what does that prove?" Megan asked.

Amelia lowered her fork to her plate and a glimmer filled her eyes. "Well," she said, "I'm glad you asked." She flexed her hands and laced her fingers on top of the table.

"Is this what you alluded to a couple of weeks ago? Before the intervention?" Kate asked. "That you figured something out?"

Amelia nodded, but it was Clara who jumped in, "Amelia, you said nothing came from the yearbook discovery. Nothing *important*."

Megan tuned out the crackling fire. The background conversations of over two dozen couples making small talk. The sound of Lake Huron at night, lapping quietly against the sand. Her eyes slid to her younger sister. Clara rubbed her fingers together near her uneaten plate of veggies. Her other thumb was drawn to her mouth, and she nibbled away at it. She was a bag of nerves, but something told Megan it had less to do with her handsome date and more to do with something in the family dynamic.

"You know what?" Megan asked, pushing her plate away and cradling her cider in her hands.

The others' eyes flew to her, Clara's face hard. Anxious.

"It's a perfect night," Megan went on, waving her hand around the dimly lit beach. "We've got the museum and new guests. Old ones. Did you notice how many are here who came to the summer event? All these people are here to have fun. Relax. Enjoy themselves."

Clara dropped her hand to her lap. Her shoulders rolled back a little. Megan looked at Kate, who now leaned into Matt, his arm draped over her shoulders.

Amelia and Michael seemed to skootch closer to one another, too.

"Why don't we do the same?"

"What?" Amelia asked. "You mean us? Take part in *Love at the Lake*?"

Megan nodded. "Exactly. No more talk about Judith. Or Dad. Or even Mom and the yearbook."

"Well, that's what I was going to tell you," Amelia protested.

Megan shook her head, blinking. "What?"

"Judith didn't enroll in St. Mary's. She was sent there. Just like Mom was."

"Who cares?" Kate cut in.

Everyone shifted their attention to Kate. Her eyes flashed.

"Yeah," Megan added. "Who does care?"

But Amelia pushed ahead. "Don't you think that means something?"

"Especially in light of the fact that St. Mary's offered a girls-only high school. For a long time, too. From Nora's enrollment clear up until the eighties, I believe," Michael said.

Megan looked from Amelia to Michael and back. Then, they themselves exchanged a look.

She saw something in them—the makings of a power couple. A rhythm. Something more than just partners in crime or boyfriend and girlfriend. She saw a passion.

"And now they are trying to reopen, though. Right, Michael?" Kate asked, her tone bored. "So what?"

"Your mother was sent to St. Mary's because she was pregnant," Michael whispered. Amelia's eyes lingered on him then she looked at the others, landing finally on Megan. A kink in her eyebrow.

"You think St. Mary's was a school for young mothers, don't you?" Megan whispered breathlessly. "You think Judith was pregnant, too?"

"Is that the problem with reopening? Was there some sort of stigma?" Clara asked.

Michael shook his head. "The lawsuit has nothing to do with it. But the thing is, they never condemned or even repurposed the old building. The old high school classroom."

"Classroom… *singular*?" Clara asked.

Amelia nodded.

Megan's interest sharpened. Maybe there *was* more to the story. Maybe, at least for some of her family, enjoying the night was more than throwing back cocktails and kicking their bare feet in the shallow water.

And maybe that was okay, too. Maybe it was okay if they kept looking for Wendell Acton. Hunting him down and finding out why he left. Where he went. And what... what in the *world* Judith Carmichael had to do with it.

If anything.

Maybe Megan needed an answer just as much as her sisters did.

CHAPTER 36—AMELIA

They continued to engage in unproductive speculation about Judith and Nora and what Michael and Amelia might learn on their trip to Heirloom. The conversation fizzled, though. Especially once they asked Matt, a veritable insider, to divulge. All he knew, however, was that he and his wife had chosen St. Mary's for no other reason than location.

"She'd have come to Birch Harbor Elementary if we lived inland," he added.

Yawns took the place of their suppositions, and Clara and Jake eventually wandered off. Megan announced that she needed to walk around and make sure there weren't any singletons lingering on the outskirts of the party. Brian joined her.

Kate and Matt stretched like an old retired couple—too old for parties. Disinterested in furthering the drama that had colored their lives for so long.

"Leaving?" Amelia asked when Kate headed toward the house, where her purse waited.

She nodded. "I reserved the attic for the girls. We don't

have beds up there yet, but they're going to have a sleepover with blankets and pillows. Keeps them from any untoward afterparties." Kate winked.

Amelia smiled. "Thanks for helping tonight, Kate. I know I sort of... fell off the wagon with things. I might have a tenant in mind for The Bungalows, though, and with Judith's endowment, I think things will even out, you know?"

"I'll keep my eye out for anyone who needs a place," Kate assured as they walked together to the house.

"Thanks."

"You guys good to handle cleanup? I'll come in the morning, but I mean for tonight."

Amelia shrugged. "I'll wrangle Michael into helping."

Kate lifted an eyebrow. "Does he need to be wrangled?"

"Oh, well..." Amelia stopped for a moment. Did Kate know? Was the conversation she and Michael had plastered across Amelia's face? She shook her head. "He always helps. It's his greatest quality, I'd say."

"I'm joking." Kate squeezed Amelia's shoulder. "You guys are great together. Even Megan thinks so."

Amelia's cheeks flushed.

Once Kate and Matt left, hand in hand, as easy and breezy as the autumn air, Amelia wrapped her arms around herself and searched for Michael.

Last she saw, he was held up by a particularly curious "Firefly"—as Megan had taken to calling her clients.

She squinted in the night, her eyes dancing from couple to couple, each huddled near a heat lamp as the temps continued to slide down, fall creeping in at full force—and somewhat early.

Amelia found Megan, who was ushering a wayward Firefly from the drinks table and over to the s'mores station, where another lonely soul awkwardly rocked from side to side as her marshmallow glowed red above the flames.

"Hey," Amelia whispered to her sister after an introduction was made and a potential match took shape.

"What's up?" Megan gestured behind Amelia to Brian, who brought two fresh cups of cider for the newly acquainted couple.

"Have you seen Michael? He disappeared on me."

Brian came up behind her. "I saw him duck inside the lighthouse. Looked like he was being hounded by a local about the Actons."

Amelia frowned. "Someone who knew my dad?"

Brian's face fell. "Oh, no. I don't think so, Amelia. Just someone whose dad worked at the lighthouse back in the day."

She walked toward the lighthouse, low-hanging Edison bulbs lighting her path until she came to the entrance. The door stood ajar, but Amelia saw no one inside. Not a curious local. Not a smitten pair of Fireflies, finding a shadow to disappear into.

About to leave, Amelia caught a flickering light coming from the staircase.

They'd decided to keep the observation deck off-limits once it turned dark. It wasn't safe, particularly for party-goers who might have opted for the *spiked* cider rather than the *spiced* cider.

Frowning, she thought back to what Brian had said. Her own observation. Michael had been cornered by one of the singles. Maybe she thought he was there as a client, too?

Brian had referred to another person. Different? The same? But then her brain reminded her of their conversation just weeks earlier.

"Michael?" she called.

No response.

Amelia glanced out the door once again then took to the stairs, climbing carefully up. Slowly. "Michael? Are you up here?"

The flickering grew more pronounced—it wasn't an overhead light or running lights. It wasn't *the* light. The bright beam that they hadn't yet tested. The one that needed maintenance first. The one that might not ever work again if Amelia couldn't find a way to steady herself. Stabilize. Settle down.

"There you are," a low voice came as she pulled herself up through the platform.

Two hands braced her elbows and before her eyes had adjusted to a floor full of glowing candles, Amelia was in Michael's arms.

In their courtship so far, the most romantic thing they'd shared was a nice dinner out. And that had been enough. So had everything he was doing to help her. All of Michael was enough. He didn't need to roll out grand gestures.

"What's all this?" Amelia glanced around then turned back to him, her confusion melting into something else.

"Amelia," Michael said, his voice unfamiliar. Quiet and soft and hesitant... so unlike the assertive edge of his lawyer persona. So unlike the academic in him. The inquisitive intellectual. The thoughtful historian.

He dropped onto the wooden planks, her hand still in his. Amelia shook her head, bewildered despite the talk. Despite the mature discussion of what the future could hold for them. Because Michael didn't believe in surprises or grand gestures. And because neither Michael nor Amelia ever considered that they might find themselves in this very position. On this very night.

And then, during Megan's *Love at the Lake* and the lighthouse's so-called grand opening that turned into less of a grand opening and more of another old Hannigan family reunion... Amelia learned that there was more to Michael than an interest in history. That there was more to her than an interest in drama.

She learned that it didn't take a great script and a dressed stage and a director to make her dreams come true.

But when she looked down, she saw more than a grand gesture. More than the candles and the observation deck where her father once stood.

She saw a thin, silver band with a delicate arrangement of tiny diamonds. It must have been a hundred years old.

Michael swallowed, the ring pinched carefully between his fingers as he looked up at her. "Amelia," he began, his voice nearly breaking, "Will you—"

"Yes," Amelia gushed, falling to the ground with him. "Where did you get this?" she whispered as she marveled at the dainty piece of jewelry, her heart pounding.

"This was my mother's wedding ring. And her mother's before her. And now, I hope it'll be yours."

Amelia frowned. "Michael," she hissed. "Are you *sure*?"

"Sure about what?" He chuckled and slid the ring onto her finger. "The ring or the proposal?"

She closed her eyes, and her dad came to mind. Or what she could remember of him. A good dad. A good husband.

And despite that, he still didn't stay.

Would Michael?

"Sure about..." Amelia's brain turned to mush, and she looked down at the ring again. They had commonalities. They had talked about this very thing. A legal arrangement. A vow.

And yet—did he really know what he was getting

himself into? Did he know that men usually broke up with Amelia? That she was flighty and unmoored?

"I'm sure about everything, Amelia. I'm sure about this. I'm sure about us. I'm sure we can find your dad if that's what you want, and you know what else?"

Tears stung the corners of her eyes. "What?"

"I'm sure that whatever happened to Wendell, he never meant to leave you and your sisters. Or your mom."

"How do you know?" Amelia managed as tears washed down her cheeks.

Michael pulled her up to her feet and cradled her head in his hands, holding her close and speaking softly. "Because no man in his right mind would ever leave you." He leaned away from her and stared hard into her eyes. "Amelia, I'm sure about *you*."

And the funny thing was? Maybe Amelia's dad wasn't in his right mind. And maybe most of her life, Amelia wasn't in hers either. But being home and having Michael... it occurred to her that, for the first time in her life, she wasn't looking for a new role. A better one. A new stage. She had everything she needed right here and now.

"Michael," she whispered back. "I'm sure, too."

CHAPTER 37—CLARA

"Where is there to go on Lake Huron?" Clara asked Jake as she settled onto the rubbery bench in the back of his boat.

Jake grinned and pushed off the dock, untethering them.

And that's exactly how Clara felt each time they were alone. Untethered. Before Jake, that feeling had only come after her mother had passed away. The free-floating sensation back then, however, was tainted with a dark void, naturally.

With Jake, though, the unknown thrilled her. Clara wasn't certain she wanted to become someone else. But she was certain she wanted to be *with* someone else.

"Are you kidding me? Where is there to go on Lake Huron—haven't you been out on the water?"

Clara shrugged and gripped the edge of her seat as they propelled off.

"You're in for a treat," he called, speeding up. The wind clouded her hearing, and she squinted into the impending sunset. They didn't have much time before it was dark, which was just as well. This wasn't a swimming date or a diving one. Not even dinner on the water, like with the ferry. It was a simple jaunt across the gentle waves. If all went well, maybe they'd extend their evening together.

He cut straight across and toward Heirloom, and Clara wondered if he wasn't also taking the opportunity to swing into the bay there, where the girls were enjoying a fun evening of their own. Vivi had invited Mercy and Sarah for a game night with their dates from Homecoming. As it turned out, Sarah declined, having her own plans with other friends.

This had given Jake a lot of anxiety, he confided in Clara. Yes, he knew that Mercy and Vivi would make good decisions and be safe. But they were only freshmen. A date night near the water made him a little nervous. But then, that's what being the father of a teenager would mean from there on out—weekend nerves.

Clara lifted her voice. "Are we swinging by Matt's?"

Jake threw his answer over his shoulder. "Nope. Just taking a loop around the Island. There's something I want you to see on the other side."

She smiled to herself and closed her eyes, wrapping her cable-knit blanket more snugly about her shoulders. Cooler temps had fallen across Birch Harbor—early, some would say. But coasting across the water as the sun sank down below the lake was nearly frigid. Or perhaps it was Clara's body temperature, bracing for some sort of impact.

They wrapped around the north side of the Island until she lost all sight of Birch Harbor.

"You must be freezing," Jake remarked, killing the engine. "Here, I'll join you." He made his way down the short distance to the bench.

Clara stood to move over, her knees weak. A shiver shook her body. Could it be a fever? But once they sank back down together, and he ran his hand up and down her back, warmth returned.

By now, kissing was an expectation. Clara's expectation, that was. Jake's too, it seemed. She leaned into him and wrapped him in her blanket as they drifted loosely yards away from an unfamiliar shoreline. The boat rocked with them, and after some moments, Clara leaned away, studying his features. Was this the face of her boyfriend? A stranger? Someone she would be waking up with years from now? Someone to grow old with? Half of her was certain it was. The other half felt like a silly girl playing with a Magic 8 Ball.

"Where do you see yourself in five years?" The question fell out of her mouth, and she wished she could pluck it from the air and pop it back inside, swallowing it down until perhaps the fifth or sixth date.

He smiled and eased his hands onto her lower back, clasping them there and steadying her. He glanced to the Island and drew his hand, indicating a barren space of shoreline. "As a matter of fact, *that's* where I see myself."

Clara squinted across the water. "What do you mean?"

"I mean I want to build a house on the Island and live there. Tide pooling is great over on this side. I could have a little dock. Mercy can come visit me when she's in town during her college breaks. It's my dream." He looked back at her.

"So, you want to stay in the area, then? No moving back to the suburbs?" She was pushing her luck, she knew.

But he shook his head. "No way. I want to be here. On the water. Besides, this is where Mercy and I have made our life. Sure, we miss how things used to be." His face darkened, and he glanced away.

Clara's breath hitched. This was it. This was the fear she had about dating a widower. A single father. He had a life outside of hers. A past. A hole in his heart that the likes of Clara Hannigan could never fill, no matter how fun she made herself or how much mascara she wore or how good a kisser she was.

She was old enough, though, to have a good answer. The right answer. Something that reassured him and validated him and set a new hope on fire for both of them, perhaps.

But all she could come up with was, "I miss my mom, too." As she said it, she cringed inwardly. Losing Nora was a complicated tragedy for Clara. But feeling bad for such an admission was wrong, too, so she just flapped her hands up and down on her thighs, her blanket falling from her shoulders.

Jake reached around her and pulled it back up. "You and Mercy have that in common, I suppose."

She blinked away an errant tear. There was no way it was good for Jake to see her in his daughter, or vice versa. She had to undo that somehow. But how could she? If the fact of the matter was that Clara had something in common with her date's daughter, she couldn't simply say *No, we are nothing alike.* But still, didn't Clara want to be a woman? A strong woman with a strong heart who was nothing like a teenager? "Well, I guess that's why we get along so well." She squeezed her eyes shut. Agreeing was undoubtedly making matters worse.

"I love that about you, Clara."

"What?" She frowned at him.

He grinned. "I just mean that it's nice to find someone

who doesn't mind that I have a daughter. That I have a past. That's one of the hard things about losing Mercy's mother. I wasn't sure if we could find a new way for ourselves, you know? A fresh start that didn't mean we'd have to pretend like she was never alive to begin with."

It was everything she needed to hear and more. Because what Jake said was that it was okay if Clara was close to his daughter. It was okay if she entered their life. And maybe, he even needed someone like her in it. Maybe there was a chance for her to fill part of his heart. Even if that little hole stayed there, it didn't mean that Clara couldn't still try to help patch it.

And maybe, Jake could help patch hers, too. After all, just as Clara could never replace Mercy's mother or Jake's wife, neither Jake nor Mercy could replace Nora. Or Kate. Or even the childhood that Clara felt so certain she'd missed.

He slid his arms around her waist and pulled her back in for a long, slow kiss, and when they came back up for air again, Clara wasn't cold anymore.

THEY ROCKED CLOSER to the shore of the Island as he talked to her about his grand plans for a little beachfront cottage, and Clara smiled at everything he said. She couldn't imagine leaving her own new home. Not anytime soon, and that took the pressure off.

"Do you spend a lot of time on Heirloom?" she asked him as he set about driving them back into town.

He nodded. "I come over a couple of times a week. Sometimes on the ferry and sometimes by myself. I've brought Mercy here, too. When we first came to town, I had looked at St. Mary's for her. I thought it might be safer for a new girl. You know?"

Clara studied the mass of land. As they skimmed along, she knew they were nearing the peppering of buildings that made up St. Mary's of the Isle and its schoolrooms. She'd been there once or twice when she was younger. One time for a fundraiser. Another for a First Communion. "Why didn't you?"

"Why didn't I enroll her?" he asked. She nodded. "I thought the teachers were a bit sharp. And Mercy didn't need that. Not then."

Clara let out a breath. "Was Judith Carmichael one of those teachers? Did you meet her at one point?" By now, Jake knew all there was to know about the Hannigan family drama. He knew too much, probably. And there was no good reason for her to bring it back up, but there she was, bringing it back up. "Oh, never mind."

He smiled at her. "You know, I don't think Judith is your woman."

Clara frowned. "What do you mean?"

"I mean, I can see that Amelia and Michael have pinned their hopes on Judith being involved, but I don't see it."

"Why not?" They crested the far side of the Island, making their way back inland. A whole night lay before them. A night of potential.

"Let me rephrase," Jake said, easing off the engine and letting them coast past the landmass and back toward town. They were a hundred yards from the house on the harbor and the dock of Clara's childhood. The one that wasn't safe to play on. The one that Nora never used but was now occupied by Matt's boat and another one. Maybe a friend's.

Maybe a guest's. "Your sisters and possibly Michael think there was some sort of foul play, right?"

Clara shrugged. She wasn't sure what they thought. But yes, it was clearly on their radar that something untoward had happened.

"But the police didn't find signs of that, right?" Jake went on.

"Well, that doesn't mean anything. It was a long time ago. Maybe we haven't found all of their reports or—" She stopped dead in the middle of her sentence. Images of the composition book in the bottom of the hope chest floated up to the surface of her mind, and she shook her head. "You're right." Swallowing, Clara forced herself to push them down. Not on their fourth date. She refused—outright refused—to derail their evening with a wild goose chase.

Jake looked over at her. She had moved to the passenger seat, the chill returning as they neared land. "Anyway," he went on, "whatever happened, it seems like things are settling. The event last night was awesome. Your sisters really know how to pull something like that off. Think they'll ever host other types of events?"

Clara dropped her chin to her chest and lifted an eyebrow at him. "What types?" In fact, yes. She had definitely considered the fact that if—and only *if*—Clara ever fell in love and chose to get married... well, now she had her sisters to help with it. She didn't have to be afraid of eloping or dealing with an overzealous Nora. She could have a normal, happy occasion.

"I'd love to put on a big Sweet Sixteen for Mercy one day," he replied.

Clara's heart sank. "Oh, yeah. That would be fun. She might like it." She shifted in her seat, tugging the blanket tightly around herself. They were closer now to the house on the harbor, so close that Clara could see in through the back kitchen windows. Matt and Kate stood there, their silhouettes ever recognizable in the glow of the sunset.

When she looked back at Jake, he was frowning. "Oh, maybe I'm wrong. I mean, it's a year away, of course, but she is shy and—"

"I know Megan would love to put a party on for Mercy. Or any of the girls." She tried for reassuring, and she tried to tamp down the notion that Jake would be thinking of a wedding on only their fourth date. This was where her youth and dreams collided into foolishness. She shook the thought and smiled back at him. "I bet we'll have lots of things to celebrate, and my sisters would love to help."

His features softened, and he started to lean across to her.

But just as their lips were about to brush, a ribbon of cold air cut between them. Clara opened her eyes, and Jake was peering suspiciously past her.

She turned and looked back at the house. Matt and Kate were gone from the window. "What is it?" she asked, alarmed.

"That buoy bell," he replied, pointing into the inky water on the far side of the boat.

She saw it in the growing dark, bobbing about like a lone ice cube. "What?"

"Its light is out."

Clara squinted at it. "I never knew those things had lights."

He shook his head. "I'll tell the office when we get in. No big deal."

Then he leaned back into her, all mundane issues melting back into Lake Huron as Clara and Jake kissed again. A fourth-date kind of a kiss. Familiar and hot, sumptuous. And Clara wondered if the very next event Megan would host wouldn't be a wedding after all.

FIND out how the Hannigan saga ends. Order Bells on the Bay *today.*

ALSO BY ELIZABETH BROMKE

Birch Harbor:

House on the Harbor

Lighthouse on the Lake

Fireflies in the Field

Cottage by the Creek

Bells on the Bay

Gull's Landing:

The Summer Society

The Garden Guild

The Country Club

Hickory Grove:

The Schoolhouse

The Christmas House

The Farmhouse

The Innkeeper's House

The Quilting House

ACKNOWLEDGMENTS

Thank you so much, Elise Griffin, for your careful eye and clever notes on how to best shape the penultimate story in the series. Sue Soares and Krissy Moran—thank you so much for your oversight and final touches!

Diane Williams, Cami Williams, and Cyndie Shaffstall: thank you for your expertise on Chapter 23. I hope I've done the diving world just a smidge of justice. And if I have, it's all thanks to you three!

As always, my family and friends are such a huge support to me. Thank you all.

My two guys and my sweet Winnie—all for you!

ABOUT THE AUTHOR

Elizabeth Bromke writes women's fiction and contemporary romance. She lives in the northern mountains of Arizona with her husband, son, and their sweet dog, Winnie.

Learn more about the author by visiting her website at elizabethbromke.com.

Made in the USA
Middletown, DE
30 September 2021